THE BABY
WHO SAVED
CHRISTMAS

THE BABY WHO SAVED CHRISTMAS

BY

ALISON ROBERTS

First published in Great Britain 2015
By Mills & Boon, an imprint of HarperCollins*Publishers*
1 London Bridge Street, London, SE1 9GF

Large Print edition 2016

© 2015 Alison Roberts

ISBN: 978-0-263-26160-8

Printed and bound in Great Britain
by CPI Antony Rowe, Chippenham, Wiltshire

For Liz
With fond memories of our visit
to Saint-Jean-Cap-Ferrat
With love

CHAPTER ONE

SOMETHING WAS GOING very wrong for Alice McMillan.

She was not supposed to be enjoying herself right now.

'I'm sorry...'

Silent, one-sided communication had become a habit even though the feeling of connection had faded over the months of this year. Now it only served to increase the prickle of guilt.

'But it *is* gorgeous... You must have loved it, too.'

All those years ago. Twenty-nine, to be exact. A period of time that had included Alice's conception.

Having stepped off the bus from Nice in the heart of the small town of Villefranche-sur-Mer, Alice crossed the road to start walking downhill, skirting around a man on a ladder who was part of the team installing a huge pattern of tinsel that would hang over the centre of the main street like a giant tiara. She'd printed off a map before leaving Edinburgh and the route looked easy enough. All she had to do was find the beach and follow it. At the other end was the start of the peninsula that was St Jean Cap Ferrat and the address she was heading for looked like it was within easy walking distance.

There was a small market happening on a grassed area opposite the bus stop. Stalls were selling things like cheese and preserves, handmade soaps and Christmas decorations. There was music coming from somewhere and the smell of hot food made her mouth water. When had she last eaten? That bag of cheese and onion crisps and a bottle of water on the last leg of her long train journey didn't really count.

She had to edge her way through a group of people who seemed to be there to socialise rather than shop but they made way for her politely and the smile of the man at the stall was welcoming.

'Bonjour, mademoiselle. Qu'est-ce qu'il vous fait aujourd'hui?'

This might be her first day ever in France but Alice had been surrounded by the sound of this language since her arrival in Paris early this morning. She'd already learned that the best response was a smile and an apology that she didn't speak French.

The apology was genuine. Most people learned at the very least to say 'please' or 'thank you' in the language of a country they chose to visit and Alice could do that in Spanish or Italian. Even Greek. But not French.

Never French...

'One of those, please.' Alice pointed to a baguette that had been split and filled with a thick slice of ham and some cheese.

'Of course.' The man switched languages effortlessly. 'You are English?'

'Scottish.'

'Ah... Welcome to Villefranche.' The sandwich was being wrapped in paper. 'You are here on holiday?'

A holiday? A place you chose to go to relax and enjoy yourself? No. This journey was definitely no holiday.

But Alice smiled and nodded as she handed over some money because the truth was far too personal to tell a stranger and too complex to explain anyway. She wasn't even sure she understood herself why she had made the impetuous decision to come here and now that she *was* here she felt like she was on an emotional rollercoaster.

It was a relief to get away from all the people. The buzz of conversation and laughter faded and the group of people she passed near the tourist attraction of the old citadel were clearly English tourists.

There was a marina below the citadel and Alice found a bench where she could sit and eat her sandwich in the afternoon sunshine. There was a man working on a boat nearby. Joggers went past and people walking their dogs or pushing prams but nobody seemed to notice Alice and she gave herself a few minutes to bask in the sunshine, enjoy the delicious fresh bread with its perfect filling and get her bearings.

She could see the curve of the beach not far away—past a line of restaurants and cafés and she could see the tongue of land that had to be St Jean Cap Ferrat. She knew the main village was out of sight, on the other side of the peninsula, but there were lots of houses on this side and one of them was the address she was heading for. Right on the coastline, in fact. If she knew where to look, she would probably be able to see it from here.

But what, exactly, did she think was going to happen when she knocked on the door? That she would only have to come face to face with this famous racing-car driver called André Laurent and he would somehow recognise her as his daughter? Or that she would show him the faded photograph she'd found hidden in her mother's most private belongings to remind him of their relationship and then disbelief would morph into amazement and finally joy?

That she would, again, have at least one person that she could think of as family?

Nerves kicked in. This had been a stupid idea. She wouldn't be welcome. It was quite likely she would have to turn around immediately and re-trace her footsteps and then what would she do? With the knowledge that the big city of Nice was so close and there was bound to be plenty of hotels, she hadn't even tried to book a room for the night or find out what time the buses stopped running.

Maybe she should just turn around now.

Alice closed her eyes and waited and, yes... there it was. That feeling that this was the right thing to do. That flicker of hope that it might even be the best thing she had ever decided to do. Okay, it was a huge gamble and it was quite possible that it would turn out to be her worst decision ever but there was only one way to find out.

And there was *something* important here.

She could feel it. A sense of...belonging?

Well, that wasn't so crazy, was it? She was half-French. She might have been brought up to dismiss this heritage as something to be ashamed of but there could be no denying that the lilt of the language around her and the feel of these streets and houses was touching a part of her she didn't recognise. A part that held whispers of content-ment. Of being *home*…

Hence the silent apology to her mother.

Jeanette McMillan would have been so horri-fied by her making this journey it was no wonder that the very idea would have been unthink-able while she was alive. Even now, Alice could hear an echo of the words that had stopped any queries about her genetic history.

'Your father was *French*…' The biggest insult ever. 'And he tried to get rid of you…'

Curiosity about even the country had to be firmly squashed because she'd loved her mother and any intermittent yearning to find out who her father might be had been something that had needed to be kept even more private, especially in recent years when her mother had already been coping with more than anyone should have to bear.

How sad was it that she would never know if her mother had loved this place as much as Alice knew she might be capable of loving it herself?

She opened her eyes again and scanned the buildings she could see more closely. Maybe the bar where her mother had been working when she'd only been eighteen was nearby. Had it had a view of this sparkling blue bay of the Mediterranean dotted with yachts or had it been tucked away amongst the ancient stone buildings on the steep, cobbled streets of the old town?

That flicker of hope ignited into tendrils of excitement. Had her mother felt this sense of freedom as she'd embarked on her first adult adventure? Alice had left it far too long to stretch her wings but how could things have been any different with first her grandmother and then her mother having to suffer through such unbearably slow and debilitating terminal illnesses?

But she was here now and everything felt new and wonderful. This hadn't been a stupid idea at all. This was magic—as if she was taking the first steps into a real-life fairy-tale. It was a shame she didn't have time to explore this historic part of the small town right now but time was marching on and it was winter. Daylight wouldn't last past about five p.m., and she didn't want to be trying to find her destination in the dark.

Her breath came out in an incredulous huff at the reminder of the season. This bright warmth was another wave of the magic wand—like the feeling of the scenery and the sound of the language was proving to be. Had it only been two days ago that Alice had been wrapped up against the bone-chilling temperatures of a Scottish winter? She'd shed her coat hours ago but still felt overdressed in her long-sleeved jumper and skinny jeans that were tucked into short boots.

The coat felt heavy over her arm as she followed the signposted walkway to the beach. It was a good thing that the few items she'd deemed necessary for a trip that might only last a day or two had fitted into a small backpack so she didn't have anything else to carry in her hands.

The beach was almost deserted, wavelets lapping at the golden sand. Even now, the sea looked inviting and Alice knew that the water temperature would probably be warmer than any beach in Scotland in midsummer. No doubt it got horribly crowded here in the high season, though, given that it was such a popular playground for the rich and famous. Didn't people like Madonna come here for holidays?

And Monaco was only a short drive down the coast. The place where her father had apparently become so famous and another Mecca for the kind of people that had always seemed like an alien race to Alice McMillan. She wasn't just visiting another country right now—it felt like she was heading for a different planet.

The path seemed to end in a car park, which was momentarily confusing, but then Alice spotted the stairs tucked against the steep bank. There was a path that followed a railway line at the top of the stairs and moments later she saw a street with a sign that gave her a name she recognised. Pulling a now crumpled map from her back pocket, Alice kept walking and it was less than ten minutes later that she came to another road that clearly led down towards the coastline again. The view back over the bay to Villefranche was spectacular but there seemed to be a downside to living on this street. There was certainly no room for anyone to park. There were vans and trucks parked nose to tail, and further down the hill she could see a large group of people milling about.

As she got closer, she could see that a lot of them were holding cameras.

Paparazzi? Was Madonna taking a winter break, perhaps? In the same street her father lived in? It wouldn't surprise her. When she'd found the street on the internet, it had looked like every house could be an exclusive resort—the dwellings massive, with huge gardens and swimming pools of Olympic size. The gates advertised just how prestigious this real estate was. Ornate black iron with gold gilding that were at least twice Alice's height, decorated with security features like cameras and intercoms. There were even security guards standing in front of the most ornate she'd seen so far. This property was also the one attracting the attention of the media. There was more than one television crew set up amongst a bank of cameras.

Disconcertingly, as Alice skirted the back of the small crowd she discovered that this was the end of the road. There were no more houses. With her heart thumping, she checked the map again. Okay, she'd known her father was famous. But *this* famous…?

The voice so close to her ear made her jump. She crumpled the map in her hand but it was too late. The man had seen the red circle and her notes and he was asking her something in a tone that was unmistakeably extremely interested.

Alice didn't bother to apologise this time. She shook her head and stepped back.

'I don't understand. I don't speak any French. Not even a single word of it.'

The man only spoke louder. And faster. He even took hold of Alice's arm and started pushing her towards the crowd.

Alice tried to pull her arm free. She had no idea what was going on but she knew she'd made a mistake now and the sooner she got away from here the better. The fairy-tale was taking an ominous twist and she needed to think about this. About taking a different approach to reach her goal, maybe.

This was frightening. Her unwelcome companion was now talking to someone else. About *her*. Her hand tightened around the ball of the map. This was nobody else's business.

How awful would it be if the media discovered that André Laurent had an illegitimate child before he did?

'It's okay,' the second man said. 'You're not in trouble. My friend is just wanting to know why you look for the house of Monsieur Laurent?'

'I…I need to talk to him, that's all. About something…important.'

'*Talk* to him?' The reporter, if that's what he was, couldn't have looked more astonished. '*Mon Dieu…* Don't you *know*?'

'Know what?'

But the two men were talking to each other again. In low voices, as if they didn't want to

be overheard. They were still attracting attention, though.

'Come with me.'

'No…I think it might be better if I come back
another time…'

But Alice was being firmly ushered forward.
Towards the gate and the uniformed guard. Another rapid conversation followed, with the second reporter providing translation.

'He wants to know who you are.'

'My name is Alice McMillan. I'm…' Suddenly,
this was terrifying. She was in a strange country and couldn't understand a word of what was
being said around her. Something was going on
and there was a grim note in the atmosphere.
How was it that she hadn't noticed the presence
of the police on the outskirts of this group? What
if she found herself in trouble simply by having
arrived in the wrong place at precisely the wrong
time?

She seemed to have unwittingly walked into
a nightmare situation and maybe the only way
through it was to be honest.

She swallowed hard. And then she stood on tip-toe and spoke quietly enough that only the security guard could hear what she said.

'André Laurent is my father.'

The phone would not stop ringing.

You would have thought that after this morning things would have settled, but there had been no sign of things calming down the last time he'd checked.

Without altering the stride of his pacing, Julien Dubois flicked a sideways glance at the floor-to-ceiling windows of the grand salon. Not that he could see more than a glimpse of the driveway between the trees edging such a private garden but he knew it led to the massive gates that locked the property away from the rest of the world. And he knew what was waiting on the other side of those gates.

What were the vultures outside the gate waiting for, exactly? A clip of a celebrity looking grief-stricken? Or better yet, *not* looking grief-stricken, which would give them permission to go digging into a background that was dripping with juicy topics.

How old was he when the mother died?

How long is it now since the tragic death of his sister?

What had caused such a family rift?

What reason could he have to hate a national icon like André Laurent so much?

Who are the people in the house with him?

What's going on?

On the other side of a room big enough to easily host a ball was a corner of the house that had a view of not only the main garden and the pool complex but a glimpse of the private beach with the background of the bay and Villefranche beyond.

Of course the owner of this house would have chosen this jewel as his man cave. The rich red of the Persian carpets was as sombre as the dark glow of the enormous mahogany desk. An entire wall was a gallery of trophies and photographs with a gilt-framed monstrosity of the man himself behind a dense spray of champagne as he celebrated one of his early wins in the Monaco race.

Julien's jaw tightened as he deliberately ignored the real reason he loathed the image but really... it was a shameful waste of a magnum of Mumm Champagne.

The muscles of the rest of his body were as tense as his jaw by the time he'd taken two steps into the room. He didn't want to be in here at all but he'd discovered it was a place that contained some particularly useful technology. Not the huge screen that had an endless loop of overpriced cars racing through the streets of Monaco. No... it was the smaller screen that provided a live feed to every security camera the property boasted. He knew which corners of the screen came from the cameras on the gateposts because checking them was becoming a half-hourly ritual.

He only needed the crowd to thin out enough and he would be able to escape a property he'd never intended setting foot inside in the first place. It wasn't as if he was getting anywhere on the mission that had brought him through the gates. It was clearly a stalemate.

The media interest didn't seem to have died down at all yet, unfortunately. And what on earth was going on right in front of the gate?

A girl looked, for all the world, as if she was *kissing* one of the security guards. No wonder he looked so shocked, stepping back and staring at her as if she was completely crazy.

Julien found himself leaning closer to the screen, as if that would help him see the image more clearly. The woman was nothing like any journalist he'd ever seen. Was it because she wasn't holding a camera or microphone? Maybe it was the odd accessory of what looked like a child's schoolbag on her back. Then she turned enough for him to see her face and he realised that his impression probably had more to do with body language than anything else. The confidence was missing. The pushiness...

Yes. She looked like a fish out of water. Bewildered even, as the guard moved further away from her, reaching for his phone.

Frightened?

The urge to offer protection was instinctive. Well honed. And quite enough to trigger a wave of a grief that he'd believed he'd come to terms with by now.

He'd tried, so hard, to keep Colette safe…

And he was failing her again, even now…

If only the tears of grief would come, they might wash away some of the anger building today but it wasn't going to happen here in this room of all places.

And it wasn't going to happen now. Not with a phone ringing yet again. And this was his personal mobile, not a house landline, which meant that it was a caller he needed to take notice of. His solicitor, probably. He'd walked out on the argument still going on in the small drawing room on the other side of the foyer but decisions had to be made about which legal documents had precedence. Was he going to win the battle he'd come here today to fight?

But this call was not a summons back to the

tense meeting. It was coming from outside the gates, from a member of his own entourage.

A glance at the screen gave him the odd feeling of a breath of wind that targeted only the hairs on the back of his neck. As he answered the call, his gaze went straight back to the security images. He could see his caller. The bodyguard his solicitor had deemed necessary for this potentially volatile visit.

'Sorry to disturb you, Monsieur Dubois.'

'What is it?'

'There's a girl here…an English girl…'

His gaze shifted fractionally. Yes, he could still see her. Just standing there, looking lost. He wasn't the only one looking her way either. In the boring hours of waiting for something newsworthy, any distraction for the reporters was probably welcome.

'And?'

'And…' The security guard muttered something incomprehensible.

'Pardon? You'll have to speak up.'

'I'm not sure that's a good idea.' On the screen, Julien could see the guard turn his back on his audience and step even further away. He spoke in a hoarse whisper that hissed over the line.

'She's saying that Monsieur Laurent is her father.'

Julien's breath came out in a derisive snort. 'Of course she is. She won't be the first to turn up with a convenient claim like that now. Send her packing.'

'But…she wants to talk to him…'

'What?'

'I know. It's bizarre but she really doesn't seem to have any idea what's going on. I thought it might be better to deal with it away from prying eyes and ears.'

Julien closed his eyes and cradled his forehead in one hand, applying pressure to both temples.

Could this day get any more complicated?

After a long silence he forced his eyes open again and let his breath out in a defeated sigh.

'Fine. Send her up to the house.'

* * *

Alice McMillan wasn't used to being the centre of attention.

It was unnerving the way she could actually feel the intense interest of the crowd of people behind her as the massive gates were opened just far enough to let her squeeze through in the company of the security guard she had whispered her secret to. She could imagine the crowd pressing closer as they shouted questions at her.

She should feel safer shut away from the pack but, if anything, Alice felt like she was falling further into a rabbit hole, like the Alice she'd been named for. Tumbling into an alien world that she was not at all sure she wanted to visit. She lifted her chin. No…this was a fairy-tale, she reminded herself. She was Cinderella and she was being escorted to the palace where the ball was about to begin.

The guard escorting her to the house was completely silent and it was a long walk. Plenty of time to look around. At a perfectly manicured garden with enough palm trees to make it look like a tropical island and citrus trees with lemons bright jewels against a glossy green background. The blue of the infinity pool was an almost perfect match for the sea it blended into, and the house…

The house looked like the kind of mansion people paid good money for the privilege of being allowed to enter. Not quite a palace but an ancient, stately villa with pillared terraces and enormous windows that probably did have a ballroom tucked away, along with a whole wing for staff quarters. It loomed ever larger as Alice walked towards it and by the time they reached the stone paving leading to the biggest front door she had ever seen, she could feel the shadow of the house settling onto her like a dark cloud that was menacing enough to suggest an imminent storm. The heavy chopping beat of a hovering helicopter overhead added to the unreality and made her feel as if she'd stepped into a movie. A modern twist on an old fairy-tale. Some kind of psychological thriller perhaps.

The guard stopped and jerked his head towards the door.

'*Allez. Il vous attend.*'

The message was crystal clear. Somebody was expecting her arrival.

Her *father*?

Oh, Lord…this was all far more dramatic than she'd ever imagined it could be. Maybe she should have paid more heed to the advice her gran had given her so many years ago.

'*Don't ever go looking for your father. You're better off not knowing…*'

Too late now. She was here and…and the door was opening, possibly by the very man she had come here to meet. Despite the hammering of her heart, Alice took a deep, steadying breath and walked on. She even summoned a smile as if that would somehow make her more welcome.

Disappointment that the wrong person had opened the door was remarkably crushing and her smile died instantly. Who was this young man who'd been sent to greet her? An employee?

Yes, that seemed most likely. A personal assistant maybe. Or a press secretary.

Someone who'd been given clear instructions to get rid of her as quickly as possible judging by the look on his face. The glare from those dark eyes, along with the fact that he was dressed from head to toe in black, made it all more sinister. A glance upwards and he then seemed to melt into the shadow of the house as he stepped back.

'Come inside, please,' he said. 'There will be photographers in that helicopter and they have very sophisticated lenses.'

His English was perfect but his accent more than strong enough to reveal his nationality. He looked French, too. Following him across an ornate foyer and through a room with a parquet floor that was easily big enough to entertain a couple of hundred people in, Alice had plenty of time to notice those superbly tailored clothes and that smoothly combed hair that was long enough to have been drawn back into a small ponytail.

She could almost hear her grandmother clicking her tongue and muttering darkly about foreigners and their incomprehensible habits but a wayward thought sneaked in that if there was any casting going on for this real-life fairy-tale, this man might have blown any competition out of the water as far as the role of the handsome prince went.

A room like a conservatory could be seen leading from the end of this ridiculously large room. Behind glass doors was a forest of indoor plants and cane furniture and beyond that Alice could see the mirror-like surface of a swimming pool. She was led towards the other side of the house, however. Into a room that was overwhelming full of...stuff. Pictures and trophies and even a wide-screen television that had a movie playing silently.

And then she saw the enormous portrait in its elaborately gilded frame and her mouth went completely dry.

This was her father's office. These were his trophies. He was probably the driver in that speeding car in the movie.

Wow... He was larger than life in every sense

in here. Supremely successful, charismatic…incredibly wealthy. Would it matter to him that she wasn't any of those things? Would he accept her for simply being his child? *Love* her even…?

The hope was so much stronger now. A happy ending was beckoning. She couldn't wait to meet him. Okay, she was nervous and knew she might be shy to start with but this meant *so* much to her. Surely he would sense that and give them a chance to explore their connection?

Her guide shut the door behind them. He walked past Alice and then turned. For a long, long moment he simply stared at her. Then he gestured towards an overstuffed chair that was probably a priceless antique.

'Take a seat.'

It was more like a command than an invitation and it ignited that rebellious streak that Alice thought she'd left behind with her schooldays. She stayed exactly where she was.

'As you wish.' The shrug was subtle. The way he shifted a large paperweight and perched one hip on the corner of the desk was less so. This was his space, the action suggested. Alice was the intruder.

Another piercing stare and then a blunt question. 'Who are you?'

'My name is Alice McMillan.' It was the first time she had spoken in his presence and her voice came out more softly than she would have liked. A little hoarsely even. She cleared her throat. 'And you are...?'

The faint quirk of an eyebrow revealed that his bad manners had only just occurred to him.

'My name is Julien Dubois. Who I am doesn't matter.'

Except it did, didn't it? He was a gatekeeper of some kind and he might have the power to decide whether her quest had any chance of success.

'Where are you from, Miss McMillan?'

'Call me Alice, please. Nobody calls me Miss— even the children in my class.'

'You are a teacher?'

'Yes. Pre-school. A nursery.'

'In England?'

'Scotland. Edinburgh at the moment but I was

brought up in a small village you won't have heard of. Where it is doesn't matter.'

Good grief...where was this urge to rebel coming from? The feeling that she'd done something wrong and had been summoned to the headmaster's office perhaps? It was no excuse to be rude enough to fling his own dismissive words back at him in exactly the tone he'd used.

That eyebrow flickered again and he held her gaze as another silence fell. Despite feeling vaguely ashamed of herself, Alice didn't want to admit defeat by looking away first. His eyes weren't as dark as they'd appeared in the shadows of the entranceway, she realised. Much lighter than her own dark brown, they were more hazel. A sort of toffee colour. He had a striking face that would stand out in any crowd, with a strong nose and lips that looked capable of being as expressive as that eyebrow, but right now they were set in a grim line, surrounded by a jaw that looked like it could do with a shave.

'And you claim that André Laurent is your father?'

The disparaging snap of his voice brought her drifting gaze sharply back to his eyes.

'He is.'

'And you have proof of this?'

'Yes.'

'Show me.'

Alice slipped the straps of her backpack from her shoulders. She sat on the edge of the uncomfortable chair to make it easier to open the side pocket and remove an envelope. From that, she extracted a photograph. It was faded now but the colour was still good enough to remind her of the bright flame shade of Jeannette McMillan's hair and that smile that could light up a room. A wave of grief threatened to bring tears and she blinked hard, focusing instead on the man in the picture. She raised her gaze to stare at the oversized portrait again.

With a nod, she handed the photograph to Julien.

'My mother,' she said quietly. 'I wouldn't have known who she was with except that she kept these magazine clippings about him.' She glanced down at the folded glossy pages still in the envelope. 'Well hidden. I only found them recently after she...she died.'

If she was expecting any sympathy for her loss it was not forthcoming. Julien merely handed the photograph back.

'This proves nothing other than that your mother was one of André's groupies. It's ancient history.'

'I'm twenty-eight,' Alice snapped. 'Hardly ancient, thanks. And my mother was not a "groupie". I imagine she was completely in love...'

'Pfff...' The sound was dismissive. And then Julien shook his head. 'Why now?' he demanded. 'Why *today*?'

'I...I don't understand.'

'Where have you been for the last week?'

'Ah...I went home to my village for a few days. And then I've been travelling.'

'You don't watch television? Or read newspapers?' He raised his hands in a sweeping gesture that her grandmother would have labelled foreign and therefore ridiculously dramatic. 'How could you not *know*?'

'Know what?'

'That André Laurent crashed his car three days ago and killed himself. That his funeral was *today.*'

'Oh, my God...' Alice's head jerked as her gaze involuntarily flicked back to the huge portrait. 'Oh...*no*...'

From the corner of her eye, she could see that Julien was following her gaze. For a long second he joined her in staring at the image of a man that was so filled with life it seemed impossible to believe that he was gone.

But then, with the speed of a big cat launching itself at its prey, Julien snatched up the paperweight from the desk and hurled it towards the portrait, creating an explosion of shattering glass, leaving behind a horrified silence that only served to magnify his chilling words.

'I wish he'd done it years ago... If he had, my sister wouldn't have married him. She would still be *alive*...'

CHAPTER TWO

THE SHOCK WAS mind-numbing.

The pain this stranger was feeling was so powerful that Alice could feel it seeping into her own body to mix with the fear of knowing that she was alone with an angry man who was capable of violence. Compassion was winning over fear, however. His sister had been married to André Laurent. Presumably she'd been in the car with him in that fatal crash. She wanted to reach out and offer comfort in some way to Julien. To touch him…?

No. That would be the last thing he would accept. She could see the agonised way he was standing with every muscle clenched so that male pride could quell the need to express emotion. With a hand shading his eyes to hide from the world.

And self-pity edged its way into the over-whelming mix.

Alice had lost something here, too.

Hope.

She'd tried to keep it under control. Ever since she'd finally found the courage to return to the cottage that had been the only real home she'd ever known because it had been time she faced the memories. Time to accept that she'd lost her only family and that she had to find a way to move forward properly from her grief. To embrace life and every wonderful thing it had to offer and to dream of a happy future.

It had been time to sort through her mother's things and keep only those that would be precious mementos.

She'd grown up in that tiny house with two women. Her mother and her grandmother. Strong women who'd protected her from the disapproval of an entire village. Women who had loved her enough to make her believe that the shameful circumstances of her birth didn't matter. That she was a gift to the world simply because she existed.

Maybe it had been a bad choice to make the visit so close to Christmastime, when the huge tree was lit up in the village square and the shops had long since decorated their windows with fairy-lights and sparkling tinsel. The sadness that this would be her first Christmas with no family to share it with had been the undercurrent threatening to wash away the new direction she was searching for, and finding that envelope that had provided the information about who her father was had given that undercurrent the strength of an ocean rip.

Had given her that hope that had exploded into something huge the moment she'd walked into this room and seen that portrait. She had been ready to love this man—her unknown father.

She'd still had a family member. Someone who'd been denied any connection with the women who had raised her but with a connection to herself that had to mean something. She was a part of this stranger.

His daughter.

It felt quite possible she had loved him already. And now she had lost him before she'd even had the chance to meet him. She would never know if there were parts of her personality she might have inherited from that side of her gene pool. Like that rebellious streak maybe. Or the unusual gurgle of her laughter that always turned heads. Her brown eyes?

Yes. Even behind the shards of broken glass clinging to the frame of that portrait and the mist of the champagne spray, Alice could see that her father's eyes were as dark as her own.

He looked so happy. Confident and victorious. And there was no denying how good looking André Laurent had been. Despite the disparaging reaction of the silent man beside her, Alice just knew that her mother had been in love and had had her heart broken. Why else had she never tried to find another relationship?

She would never even discover whether André remembered her mother. If she had, at least, been conceived in love on both sides.

Yes. That hope of finding something that could grow into a new but precious version of family was gone. It was dead and had to be buried. Like her father had been only this morning.

Her breath hitched and—to her horror—Alice felt the trickle of tears escaping.

And then she heard a heavy sigh.

'*Je suis désolé*. I'm sorry.' Julien's voice had a very different timbre than she had heard so far. Softer. Genuine? Whatever it was, it made his accent even more appealing. 'I should not have done that.'

Alice swallowed the lump in her throat. The fear had gone. This man wasn't violent by nature. He had just been pushed beyond the limits of what anyone could bear. She knew what moments of despair like that could feel like.

'It's okay,' she said, in barely more than a whisper. 'I understand. I'm very sorry for your loss.'

The response was a grunt that signalled it was not a subject that he intended to discuss any further.

Alice was still holding the photograph of her

parents. It was time to put it back in the envelope, along with the clippings that had supplied the name missing from her birth certificate. She slipped the envelope into the side pocket of her backpack and zipped it up. Then she picked up the straps to put it back on.

'Where are you going?'

Alice shrugged. 'I'll find somewhere. It doesn't matter.'

Julien moved so that he was between her and the door. 'You can't go out there. You can't talk to those reporters. They would have a—what do you call it? A…paddock day with a story like this.'

There was a faint quirk of amusement to be found in the near miss of translation. 'A field day.' She shook her head. 'I won't talk to anyone.'

'They'll find out.' Julien's headshake was far sharper than her own had been. 'They'll discover who you are and start asking questions. Who else knows about this…claim of yours?'

Alice was silent. What did it matter if he didn't believe her? Nobody else knew anything more than what had been impossible to hide. That her mother had gone to work for a summer in the south of France. That she had come home alone and pregnant.

'Do you have any idea what the Laurent estate is worth?' Julien's gaze flicked over her from head to foot, taking in her simple, forest-green jumper, her high-street jeans and the well-worn ankle boots. The backpack that dangled from her hands. 'No…I don't suppose you do.'

He was rubbing his forehead with his hand. Pressing his temples with long, artistic fingers that made Alice wonder what he did for a living, which was preferable to feeling put down by her appearance. Was he a surgeon, perhaps, or a musician? The black clothes and the long hair fitted more with a career in music. She could almost see him holding an electric guitar—rocking it out in front of a crowd of adoring fans…

'I need to get advice.' Julien sounded decisive now. 'Luckily, I have my solicitor here in the house with me. And I expect a DNA test will soon sort this out.'

'There's no point now.'

'Pardon?'

'I came here to meet my father. If he'd needed that kind of proof I wouldn't hesitate but it's… too late now. It doesn't matter because I'm never going to meet him, am I?'

'But don't you want to know?'

Did she? Maybe it would be better to find out that André Laurent *wasn't* her father, however remote that possibility was, because then she could walk away knowing that she hadn't lost something that had been real and so close to being within her grasp.

And if he was, she wouldn't be haunted by knowing that her father was still out there in the world somewhere but impossible to find. She knew in her heart that she was right but there was something to be said for having written confirmation of some things, wasn't there?

So Alice shrugged. 'I guess so.'

'Come with me.' Julien opened the door. 'I do not want to be in this room a second longer.'

With what was probably going to be her last glance at her father's portrait, Alice followed him out of the office. She expected to traverse the length of the enormous room again but, instead, Julien stayed at this end of the house and threw open the glass doors to the conservatory. He waited for her to enter, his face expressionless. Perhaps the effort of keeping that anger under control left no room for anything else.

Even a hint of a smile would do.

The memory of that soft tone in his voice when he'd apologised was fading. Oddly, Alice wanted to hear it again. Or to see something that would suggest it had been genuine. That she was correct in thinking that she'd caught a glimpse of the real person buried under this grim exterior. A person she had, for an instant of time, felt a connection with.

But his tone was just as empty as his face. All that was left was the accent that still tickled her ears and made her feel as if there was a secret smile hovering just over her lips, like a butterfly waiting to alight.

'Have a seat,' he said. 'Are you hungry? I can ask the housekeeper to provide something for you.'

'No. Thank you. I had lunch not long ago.'

'As you wish. I shouldn't be too long. Please, wait here.'

She didn't really have a choice, did she? She could walk out of the house but those security guards wouldn't open the gates without getting permission and even if it was given, she would then face the media pack and…and she'd always been hopeless at lying.

Probably thanks to her father's genes, Alice had failed to receive more than the blue eyes that every member of the McMillan clad had had. She had been quietly thankful that she had escaped the flaming red hair that ran through generations of her mother's family. It hadn't been banished entirely, but her version was a rich auburn instead of orange. It was a shame she'd missed the olive skin that had been evident in that portrait of her father, though. She had pale, Scottish skin—inclined to freckle with any sunshine and turn a bright red when she blushed.

Which was what she always did if she tried to tell a lie.

Walking between the cool green fronds of huge, exotic ferns in tall terracotta urns, Alice headed for a cane couch with soft-looking, cream upholstery. Unbidden, a memory surfaced that provoked a poignant smile.

She had been about four years old and she'd done something bad. What had it been? Oh, yes… She'd been rebellious even then and she had gone to play somewhere she hadn't been allowed to go alone—behind the hen house and down by the creek. Knowing that the mud on her shoes would reveal her sin, she had taken them off and hidden them under a bush. When the query had come about their whereabouts, tiny Alice had given innocence her best shot and she'd said she didn't know where her shoes were. The fairies must have taken them.

Her mother and her grandmother had simply looked at each other.

'She's blushing, Jeannie. She's no' telling the truth.'

'Aye…'

And then the two women who'd ruled her universe had turned their gazes on Alice. She'd never forgotten what that silence felt like as they'd waited for her to confess. The guilt and the shame of it. They'd never had to wait that long again.

Not that she had any intention of confessing to any reporters but Julien was probably right. They already knew her name because they'd been right there when she'd introduced herself to the security guard. It wouldn't take long for them to chase down a story and if she was confronted by leading questions, her skin would betray her.

She could feel a prickle of heat in her neck, just *thinking* about having to lie.

At least she was safe here. The world outside those gates could be as far away as her home as she sat here in this quiet space amongst the greenery, looking out over the reflection of palm trees on the swimming pool. Her gaze was automatically drawn further—to where the water fell over the end and made it look as if the cruise ship in the distance was sharing the same patch of ocean.

And then Alice felt a shiver dance down her spine. The atmosphere had changed as noticeably as if a cool breeze had blown through the room. She didn't have to turn her head to know that Julien had returned.

Maybe she didn't feel so safe in here after all.

She was sitting on one of the couches, looking out at the view.

Julien could only see her profile but it made him realise he hadn't really looked at her until now. Or rather he'd looked at her as simply another issue that had to be dealt with on one of the darkest days of his life.

Now he could see her as media fodder and wouldn't they have a feast? This Alice McMillan was tiny. A few inches over five feet perhaps and slim enough to wear children's clothing. That bag she was carrying looked like an accessory to a school uniform.

And there was no denying how pretty she was. That tumble of richly coloured, wavy hair... Given how unpretentious the rest of her clothing was and the fact that her nails weren't even painted, it was highly likely the colour was natural and it all added up to a brand of woman that Julien had no idea how to handle due to an almost complete lack of experience. Even his own sister had morphed into one of the polished beauties that every man wanted to be seen with. Did other men always have that nagging doubt about how genuine they really were?

The memory of tears slipping from chocolate-brown eyes that had reminded him of a fawn made him groan inwardly. Imagine how that would go down in a television interview. She would have the whole world on her side.

André Laurent and—by association—his sister and then he himself would be branded as heartless rich people who were uncaring of an impoverished relative. If, of course, her claim was true. And why wouldn't it be? Given the endless stream of women in that man's life, the probability of a legacy like this was certainly believable and, according to the legal expert he'd just been speaking to, the implications were enormous. He kept his tone light enough not to reveal the can of worms that was potentially about to be opened, however.

'The news is good,' he said. 'We have made some enquiries and apparently there have been great advances in DNA testing and a result can be found within a matter of a few days. All we need is a simple mouth swab from you. Someone is coming to the house soon, to do what is needed.'

She nodded slowly and then bent her head, a thick curl of her hair falling across her cheek. She pushed it back as she looked up again.

'But they would have to match it, wouldn't they? It's too late to get a sample from my...from André. Monsieur Laurent,' she added quickly, as though she didn't have the right to be so familiar.

'M'sieur.' Without thinking, Julien corrected her pronunciation to make the 'n' silent. She really didn't know a word of French, did she? Then he shrugged. 'It seems that there are many items that may suffice. Like his toothbrush. Someone is coming who is an expert. He works with the police.'

'The *police*?' A look of fear made her eyes look huge against that pale skin.

It was like that moment after he'd hurled the paperweight at the image of the man he'd despised so much and he realised he'd scared her enough to make her cry. A shameful thing. He didn't treat women like that. He didn't treat *anyone* like that. This whole disaster was turning him into a person he really didn't like and this woman was making it that bit harder to sort out the issue that was so personally—and urgently—important. This made her someone he needed to remove from his company at the earliest opportunity so it shouldn't matter at all how she was feeling.

But it did.

It made him want to reassure her. Comfort her even.

He turned away so he didn't get trapped in those eyes. He shrugged off the unwelcome sensation that something very private was being accessed. Like his heart? How long had it been since he'd felt the urge to protect a woman? Maybe he'd given up on trying to care after Colette had made it so clear he'd been wasting his time. That he didn't understand. All those years and, in the end, they had counted for nothing.

'A coincidence,' he said, the words coming out more sharply than he might have chosen. 'This man also runs a private paternity testing company.' A sigh escaped that had a whisper of defeat about it. The need to reassure was too powerful. 'You are not being accused of anything.'

Yet, he added silently. But then he made the mistake of looking at her again. No. She wasn't here to chase five minutes of fame or a share in a vast fortune. There was no mistaking her sincerity. Or her vulnerability. She not only believed that André was her father, it held a huge significance for her. It had to be simply another coincidence that she had arrived with such unfortunate timing.

It could be an hour or more before the DNA expert arrived from Nice with his testing kit and it would be extremely impolite to leave her waiting here alone and it would be imprudent to antagonise her. For everybody's sake, this matter had to be kept as private as possible.

'So...' Julien lowered himself onto a couch facing Alice. 'You are a teacher?'

'Yes.'

'You like children, then?'

'Of course.'

'Do you have any of your own?'

That startled her.

'No...I'm not...um...married.'

'Neither was your mother.'

Maybe she wasn't quite as vulnerable as he'd thought. A flash of something like anger crossed her face and her chin lifted.

'She suffered for that. There are communities where it's still considered shameful to produce an illegitimate child.'

Julien blinked. If the mother had suffered, it was logical to assume that the child had as well.

'Why did she go back, then?'

The stare he was receiving made him feel like he'd asked a very stupid question. There was something even more disturbing in that look, however. Pity? Was he missing something fundamental?

'Brannockburn was her home. She was very young and her heart was broken. She needed her mother.'

A broken heart? Well, she probably hadn't been the only woman who'd believed that she might be the one to tame André Laurent. He could hardly brand her as a complete fool when his own sister had fallen under the same spell decades later.

'I'm sorry...' Her apology was unexpected.

'What for?'

Alice was twisting a lock of hair in her fingers as she shifted her gaze to the doors that led back into the house. 'You've lost your sister. You must have family here. Your mother perhaps? I'm intruding on a very personal time. I'm sorry. Obviously, I wouldn't have come if I'd had any idea of what had happened.'

'My only family was my sister,' Julien said quietly. 'And I lost her three months ago. She died in childbirth.'

* * *

A heavy silence fell but Alice didn't dare look back at him.

Had the baby died as well? Had they both recently lost their only living relatives? Not that there was any real comparison. He'd known his sister and she'd only lost the potential of knowing her father. But she knew what it was like to lose the person who was the emotional touchstone in one's life. Her mother had seemed far too young to be taken but how old had Julien's sister been? Probably only in her thirties, as he looked to be himself.

This was a tragedy in anybody's terms and Julien clearly blamed her father and hated him for it. She had come here claiming a close relationship to André so it was no wonder she wasn't welcome. Had André been as reckless on public roads as he'd been on a racing circuit? That would give credence to the idea that the crash had been his fault but Julien had said his sister had died in childbirth months ago. How could André be blamed for that?

A cold chill ran down Alice's spine. Had it been an abortion that had gone horribly wrong? That was part of her own history, in a way. The only reason she existed had been because her mother had refused to go along with what had been deemed compulsory.

The silence grew heavier. And more awkward.

And then it was broken by something totally unexpected.

The wail of a baby.

CHAPTER THREE

ALICE FOUND HERSELF staring at the doors as the sound grew louder. Julien had gone pale. He got to his feet and walked past her without a word. Without thinking, Alice stood up and followed him.

There seemed to be two groups of people at the other end of the huge room. Two men wearing dark suits, facing each other and talking loudly. Behind the second man were two women. One was older and wore an apron. A younger woman was carrying the baby, who couldn't be more than about three months old. The age of the youngest of the children who attended the pre-school educational centre she worked for.

The age Julien's nephew or niece would have been by now?

Julien was walking swiftly, as though he intended to stop them coming any further. Alice was a few steps behind by the time they all stopped.

They spoke French, of course, so she couldn't understand a word but she could pick up a sense of what was going on. There was a problem of some kind and Julien wanted nothing to do with it. She couldn't be sure that he'd even looked at the baby, having positioned himself alongside one of the men so that he was only facing the other man and the older woman. Their voices rose over the sound of the baby crying and the younger girl was looking ready to cry herself.

Alice might teach the older pupils at the Kinder-care Nursery School but she had had enough experience with the youngest children to know that this baby wasn't well. The crying was punctuated by coughing. He had a runny nose and kept rubbing at his eyes with a small fist. His mother, if that's who she was, jiggled the bundle she held with what looked like a desperate attempt to comfort him. When she looked away from the heated discussion happening between the others, she met Alice's gaze and there was a plea in that look that Alice could not ignore.

She moved closer, her arms outstretched in an invitation to give the mother a break from a stressful situation. Astonishment gave way to relief as Alice took the baby, unnoticed by anyone else. She walked away, back towards the conservatory, with the thought that she could at least give them a chance to talk without having to shout over the wailing, which was probably becoming a vicious cycle as the loud voices distressed the baby further.

'It's okay, sweetheart,' she told the baby. 'You're just miserable, aren't you? Look, it's cooler in here. Let's get that blanket off you and let you cool down, shall we?'

The tone was one she used with any unhappy child and her movements were calm and confident as she unwrapped the covering that would be far too hot for a baby who was probably running a temperature.

'You've got a cold, haven't you?' Spikes of damp, dark hair covered the baby's forehead and Alice smoothed them back. 'They're rotten things, colds, but you know what?'

The exaggeration of her question seemed to have finally caught the baby's attention. He hiccupped loudly and opened his eyes to look up at Alice.

Dark eyes that had that baby milkiness that made it hard to decide whether they were blue or brown.

'Colds go away.' Alice smiled. 'In a day or two you're going to feel ever so much better.'

She unsnapped the top fastenings of the sleep suit to allow a bit more fresh air to cool the baby's skin. Miraculously, he'd stopped crying now, so Alice rocked him gently and started singing softly. It was amazing how comforting it was to hold this tiny person. For the first time Alice felt as if she was welcome in this house.

Needed even.

The baby's eyes drifted shut and only moments later there she was sitting in the conservatory again but this time holding a sleeping infant.

A quiet one.

For a few seconds Alice watched the baby's face as it twitched and settled deeper into sleep. Who was he? Julien's child perhaps? Was that young woman his wife? Or his girlfriend perhaps, given the speed with which he'd suggested it wasn't necessary to be married to have a child. If either scenario was correct, her opinion of him was dropping rapidly. He should have been trying to help, not making things worse.

Not that she could hear the sound of any arguments any more.

In fact, it was so quiet she glanced up with the worrying thought that they might have all gone somewhere else and left her with the baby.

To her horror, she found that there were five people watching her from the doorway.

Julien looked angry again. His words were cold.

'What, exactly,' he bit out, 'do you think you are *doing*?'

Wasn't it obvious? Alice said nothing. The younger woman was standing with her head down as if she knew she had done something wrong. Julien said something and she started to move towards Alice but then the older woman halted her with a touch on her arm and spoke. Another discussion started amongst the group with rapid, urgent-sounding words.

At the end of their conversation the two women and the men turned and walked away. Alice knew her face would be a question mark as Julien turned back but he didn't meet her gaze.

'It seems that this is the first time the baby has slept in many hours. It would be to his benefit not to disturb him for a little while.'

'He's not well. I think he's running a temperature.'

'A doctor has been summoned.'

Julien stopped his pacing amongst the greenery with his back towards Alice.

Alice broke the silence. 'What's his name?'

'Jacques.'

'Is he your son?'

Julien turned very slowly and his expression was…shocked. Appalled even—as if the very idea of having a child was the worst fate he could imagine.

'Of course not.'

Alice frowned. 'Then why is he here? Whose baby is he?'

Julien closed his eyes. 'My sister's.'

It was Alice's turn to be shocked. That made him Julien's nephew. An orphan who had only just lost his father and was in desperate need of any remaining family. But Julien didn't seem to want anything to do with little Jacques. Because he was also André's son?

Oh… Another shock wave rocked Alice. If André *was* her father, then that made this baby her half-brother.

Part of her own family…

She loved children anyway and would do anything to help one who was in distress but her compassion towards this infant had just morphed into something much bigger. Something totally unexpected and potentially hugely significant.

She stared at the sleeping infant's face, the dark fan of eyelashes over cheeks that were too red.

A patchy kind of red, like a rash of tiny spots. Even asleep, his tiny hands were in fists and he still felt too hot. The patch of skin she had exposed by unbuttoning the sleep suit was also red. Spotty, even.

The mind-blowing implications of a genetic relationship were pushed aside. Alice pulled open the suit a little further. Yes…the rash was everywhere. Faint but unmistakeable.

'Oh, no…'

'What?'

She looked up to find Julien had stepped closer. It was the first time she'd seen him look directly at the baby and it was a fleeting glance, almost as if he was afraid of what he might see. Perhaps he had good cause to feel afraid…

'I thought he only had a cold,' Alice said. 'But…but this looks like it might be measles.'

'How do you know?'

'I've seen a lot of pictures. There was an outbreak in Edinburgh last year and we had a lot of our children absent because of the quarantine necessary. One of them had an older sister at school who got very sick.'

'Quarantine?'

'Measles is a notifiable disease in most countries. It's highly contagious and it can be dangerous. The girl I was talking about got one of the worst complications—encephalitis—and she… she died.' Alice paused to draw in a breath. 'Even one case and anybody who's been within possible contact has to be quarantined for about two weeks. Unless they've been immunised or have had measles themselves.'

'Have you had measles?'

'Yes. When I was a child. Have you?'

'How am I supposed to know something like that?'

'From health records perhaps. An immunisation card that your mother would have kept.'

He shook his head. 'I don't know of anything like that.' He had taken a step back, as if that was enough to protect himself, and that bothered Alice. She cuddled Jacques a little closer.

'You've been in the same house,' she said, rubbing in the unwelcome information. 'The same room. Contacts can spread measles before they start feeling sick themselves. There was a case in the States last year where everybody was placed in isolation because they'd been sitting in a doctor's waiting room where there'd been a case of measles earlier that day.'

Julien shook his head again, more slowly this time. 'That is not going to happen here. It cannot. The situation is difficult enough as it is.' He took another step back. 'It's not as if I've touched the child.'

Alice felt a stirring of real anger. Why *not*? This baby had never known his mother and his father had died days ago. Had there only been hired help to offer comfort? He wasn't even looking at Jacques again now. As if he could make the problem disappear by ignoring it. And then he spoke again, on the end of a sigh.

'I have been forbidden to see Jacques,' he said. 'Ever since my sister died. But she made me his guardian and that is why I'm here today. To collect him.'

It still made no sense. 'But you still haven't *touched* him? Seen him even?'

'The Laurent family have another court order. His grandmother is arriving later today also with the intention of taking guardianship of Jacques. That is why the solicitors are here. It is a very delicate situation. My solicitor advised me not to make things worse and…for me…'

He *was* looking at Jacques now. With an expression that broke Alice's heart.

'For me, I knew it would only make things so much harder if I saw him and then…he was taken away.'

So he really *did* care.

Any anger Alice was feeling towards Julien evaporated. She had no idea why he'd been refused contact with his nephew after his sister had died but, whatever the reason, it had to be unfair. Cruel, in fact. If there were sides to be taken in this dispute, she had just put herself firmly on Julien's side.

The impression lasted only for a heartbeat. Julien's almost desperate expression vanished as his attention was caught by something he heard. He turned his head towards the windows.

'Someone is arriving,' he announced. 'Let's hope it is the doctor, who can sort this out. Let's hope that you are wrong.'

Or was it the DNA expert who had been summoned to sort out the other problem that was pending? Was he hoping she was also wrong about who she thought her father was?

To Alice's relief, the doctor looked like a kindly man. Grey-haired and a little overweight, with deep smile lines around his eyes—a quintessential family GP. He came into the conservatory accompanied by the two women.

The older woman went to take the baby from her arms and he whimpered the moment as she touched him. Alice rocked him again. She didn't want to let him go.

'Shh,' she whispered. 'It's okay, little one. We all want to help you.'

He cried out more loudly when the woman touched him for the second time and the doctor cleared his throat and then spoke in excellent English.

'Perhaps it's better if the baby stays with you while I examine him, *mademoiselle*. He seems to like you.'

Alice nodded. Was it too far-fetched to imagine that the baby was aware of a connection between them? Or maybe it was because she knew how unwelcome *she* was in this house as far as Julien and probably any other members of the household were concerned. This baby had no idea of the trouble she was causing and now he was causing trouble himself, poor little thing, so there *was* a connection to be found quite apart from any yet-to-be discovered genetic one. They were both problems. He needed protection, this little one, and she was just the person to provide it.

She held the baby while the doctor took his temperature and listened to his heart and lungs. She helped him undress the baby down to his nappy so that he could see his skin. Jacques whimpered miserably at the disturbance.

'He needs paracetamol, doesn't he?' Alice asked the doctor. 'And sponging with lukewarm water?'

'Indeed. You are familiar with nursing children?'

'I'm a pre-school teacher. We often have to deal with sick children and I've done some training. I've never dealt with a case of measles, though. Is that what it is?'

'It would seem very likely. He has all the symptoms, including Koplik's spots inside his cheeks. Are you immune?'

'Yes. I had measles as a child.'

'Do you have documentation to prove your immunity?'

'No…' Alice closed her eyes on a sigh. The need for such documentation would never have occurred to her as she'd embarked on this impulsive journey.

'Are you aware of how serious this is?'

She nodded. 'I've kept up with news of outbreaks since we had a scare in Edinburgh.'

'Then you'll know that a case has to be reported

and that there are very strict isolation and quarantine procedures that must be followed. I need to offer immunisation and prophylactic treatment to everybody who cannot prove their immunity.'

Julien had been standing within earshot. 'Quarantine is completely out of the question for me. I am due in Paris for filming in the next day or two. It's a Christmas show that's been planned for many months and cannot be postponed.'

The doctor sighed. 'I know who you are, Monsieur Dubois—of course I do. My wife is one of your biggest admirers but...' he raised his hands in a helpless gesture '...rules cannot be broken, I'm afraid. Not when it could put the health of so many others at risk.'

Alice blinked. The doctor looked to be in his sixties and his wife was one of Julien's biggest fans? If he wasn't in an edgy rock band, what sort of music did he produce? Romantic French ballads perhaps, with the accompaniment of an acoustic guitar? Was he doing a collection of Christmas carols for a seasonal show? No. Somehow it didn't fit—especially right now, with that angry body language.

With a sound of pure frustration Julien pulled a mobile phone from his pocket and walked away as he held it to his ear. The doctor turned to the two women and began speaking in French again.

Concerned expressions became horrified as he kept talking. The younger woman burst into tears. Voices rose as panicked questions were asked. Behind her, Alice could hear Julien also raising his voice on his telephone call. Everybody was sounding upset and all Alice could do was to sit there and hold the baby. It was the doctor who finally noticed that Alice was being completely left out of the conversation.

'Marthe—the housekeeper here—has grandchildren at home and she's worried,' he explained. 'Nicole—Jacques's nanny—has much younger siblings that she visited only yesterday. They are both very scared and want to take their quarantine periods in their own homes. This is possible, as their contacts will also have to be isolated. I will be visiting their households as soon as I leave here.'

Alice looked down at the baby she was still

holding. And then she looked up at the doctor and nodded her head. 'I can look after Jacques.'

'I can see if there is a nurse available who is prepared to come into the house for the quarantine period but I doubt that any arrangements could be made until tomorrow. It would be very good if you could care for him until then.'

Julien snapped his phone shut. 'No,' he said. 'Mademoiselle McMillan cannot stay in this house. She will have to find a hotel.'

'That would be the very worst thing she could do. This is a very serious matter, Monsieur Dubois. I can take a blood sample from her but it may take a few days to prove immunity and even then she may be discouraged from leaving the house.'

'You don't understand. There's another matter that is pressing.'

'Oh?'

Julien turned his gaze to Marthe and Nicole, who were whispering together near the doorway, looking desperate to escape and get back to their own families. A few words from Julien and they both disappeared.

Julien continued speaking in French to the doctor, who blinked in astonishment as his gaze settled on Alice. She could feel the prickle of a blush starting. Any moment now and the colour of her cheeks would rival that of Jacques's.

There was sympathy in the doctor's smile when Julien had stopped speaking.

'You are having quite a day, my dear, are you not?'

'Mmm...' The kind tone almost undid her but Alice was not going to cry in front of Julien again.

'The reason you came here is not important right now. What matters is that you *are* here and we are lucky that you have experience with young children. Or maybe it's more than lucky.' There was compassion in this kindly doctor's eyes. This was a man who'd spent a lifetime caring for people who were sick and vulnerable. Who had a wealth of understanding of the intricacies of human relationships. 'It could be that you are this little one's big sister, yes?'

Alice nodded slowly, her throat suddenly too tight to swallow. The tears were harder to hold back now. She would have stepped up to care for this baby no matter who he was, but the idea that she had a member of her own family who desperately needed her help was overwhelming.

She had come to this place to try and find the only living relative she might have.

This might be a bizarre twist to her fairy-tale but it seemed like she might have actually achieved her goal. And it came with an entirely new world of hope.

And, for one night at least, she could hang onto that hope.

The doctor patted her shoulder. 'Tomorrow will be a new day. In the meantime, I will leave you all the medications you might need. Here, let's give him his first dose of paracetamol and then I will take the blood samples I need from you and Monsieur Dubois.'

It was Julien's turn first. And then it was

Alice's turn and she couldn't free an arm while she was still holding Jacques.

She looked at Julien.

The doctor looked at Julien.

It was crystal clear what the logical solution was but Julien seemed frozen. Alice could sense his fear. He'd never touched this baby. Was he afraid that he would drop him or was his reluctance due to something deeper? An even harder barrier to overcome?

She could hear the echo of those heart-breaking words.

'...it would only make things so much harder if I saw him and then...he was taken away.'

Touch was a far more powerful sense than sight, wasn't it?

But he cared. And, like herself, Jacques was his relative. Was he feeling the same kind of overwhelming connection that she was?

He had more right than she did to feel like that. More right than she did to know the joy of cuddling this small person.

Slowly, she walked towards Julien. She held his

gaze, trying to offer both reassurance and encouragement. When she was so close that the baby was touching them both, his arms came up. So slowly. And then she felt the weight being transferred and Julien's gaze dragged itself away from hers and dropped to the face of his tiny nephew. He turned away then, as though he wanted to keep this moment private.

Mon Dieu...

How shocking was this?

The first time he had touched his sister's child.

He'd had no choice but to back away from any desire to see his nephew while André had still been alive. Even today, in the hours he'd known he was in the same house, it had been easier to comply with the legal advice to keep his distance. Maybe he'd known what he would feel in this moment. This emotional connection. The vulnerability of a tiny being that would suck him into offering not only his protection but his love. A breeding ground for feelings of guilt and worry and love that might eventually be thrown back at him as not having been good enough, but nothing could prevent him from providing any of it. He already loved this nephew despite trying to hide from that knowledge. He'd never intended being in this position again. He didn't know if he was strong enough.

But, once again, it seemed that he had no choice and he'd come here to do what his sister had asked him to do—to take guardianship of his child if anything happened to her. And now that he was holding him, how could he ever let him go? If he lost the legal battle with Madame Laurent, it was going to haunt him for the rest of his life.

The baby's eyes were wide open. Perhaps he was as shocked as Julien was at this unexpected physical contact. Could babies sense what people were thinking? Did he know he presented a threat out of all proportion to his size?

Maybe he did. Maybe he wanted to be back in the embrace of Alice's arms. How strange was it that she had been the only person able to comfort him in his misery? Did he sense the likely connection between them? A half-sister was a closer relation than an uncle.

Dark eyes stared up at him, making Julien wonder again how much was being understood. Too much, it seemed. The tiny face began to crumple. The small body squirmed like a fish that had been landed and needed to get back to the water to survive. And then that dreadful, unhappy wailing began again.

He paced back and forth as he waited for Alice to swap the ball of cotton wool she was pressing to her elbow for a plaster. He watched the doctor pack his things back into his bag and heard him say that he would deal with all the precautions needed for everybody who would be leaving the house to enter quarantine in their own homes—including the solicitors. He saw him leave and knew that in a very short space of time he would be alone in this house with Alice McMillan.

And still the baby was crying. More quietly, though. An exhausted sound of misery.

And there was a terrible smell. It was the odour that was really the final straw. Julien's sense of smell and taste were finely honed. They had to be to be as good at his work as he was and this... this was making him feel decidedly ill.

He needed help.

The doctor had been right. It really was very lucky that Alice was not to be allowed to leave the house.

Julien did his best to summon a smile as he moved closer. Preferably one that was apologetic. She hadn't bargained on any of this when she'd come to this house, had she? He'd not only been rude to her, he'd been violent in front of her and now she was as much of a prisoner here as he was, at least until the results of those blood tests came back. She had every right to be angry with him. To refuse to help even.

The smile came out a bit broken and he knew he was frowning fiercely so he had to say something.

'Alice...' The tone of her name came out as a plea that made him wince inwardly but this was a moment when he simply had to swallow his pride. 'I think that I...need your help. *Please...*'

CHAPTER FOUR

IT WAS SOMEWHAT startling to discover that she really liked this man.

Maybe it was the way he said her name, with an inflection and accent that made it sound so much more exotic. More like *Elise* than Alice.

Maybe it was the desperate edge to the word 'please'.

Or maybe it was the expression in his eyes. This was not someone who was used to feeling out of control of any situation and he was hating every second of this but he was too emotionally exhausted to fight any longer. Of course he was. He'd been dealing with who knew how much grief and hatred and mistrust, maybe even fear, all in the space of the short time Alice had been there?

It wasn't that she felt obliged to help. She would

have gladly cared for Jacques without anybody even asking. He was her brother, for heaven's sake.

But now her heart went out to Julien in spite of everything. She wanted to help *him* just as much.

Silently she held out her arms and took the baby. She couldn't help screwing up her nose.

'Phew... He needs a clean nappy.'

Julien nodded. He was taking a step back, the way he had when he'd heard about the possibility of measles.

'Where's the nursery?'

'I have no idea.'

Alice kicked herself inwardly as she remembered that he'd never been allowed to see his nephew so, of course, he hadn't visited this house. There was a lot more going on here than she had any knowledge of. Undercurrents that were powerful and dark.

Through the glass walls of the conservatory she could see cars leaving. The doctor's car with the housekeeper and the nanny. Then two other cars that presumably held the men in suits. The idea that the three of them were now alone in this vast house should have been alarming but this was simply another twist in the strangest day of her life and Alice felt curiously calm.

Thankfully, Jacques was settling in her arms, with just an occasional hiccup to let them know he still wasn't happy. She took a slow, inward breath as she shifted his weight to hold him more comfortably.

'Let's go and find it, then, shall we?' She offered a tentative smile with the suggestion. She might be the one who knew what to do but she didn't want to be left to do it entirely by herself. It felt as if she was doing something wrong, taking over the house of complete strangers, let alone taking over the care of their child. 'I expect it will be upstairs somewhere?'

Alice could sense Julien's hesitation so she held eye contact. Her message was silent but firm.

There's only the possibility that this baby is my brother. He's definitely your nephew. I know you think it might make things harder for you but you know what the right thing to do is...

His nod was so subtle she wouldn't have picked up on it if she hadn't been deliberately attempting a bit of telepathy.

And maybe there was a silent message coming back in her direction.

I know. I'll try...

Nothing was said aloud and, with Jacques now drowsy, it was in complete silence that they both left the huge room. The foyer was much bigger than Alice had noticed when she'd first come in. Had she not even looked up to see the gallery of the second floor that ran around three sides of this incredibly high, square space? No. She'd been focused on the fact that the man who'd greeted her was far too young to be her father. On his dark clothing and the ponytail that would have made her grandmother shake her head disapprovingly.

It didn't bother Alice. In fact, she quite liked it. There was no doubt that Julien was a very good-looking man and the smoothness with which his hair was combed back made it look as elegant as his clothing, but the short tail had a curl to it. Did he wear it loose when he was performing? Did it frame and soften his face and brush his shoulders in soft waves?

She'd quite like to see that...

The brief distraction of her train of thought vanished as she let her gaze roam the towering space. It was too much like a museum to feel like a home. The floor was marble and there were pillars supporting scalloped archways that were echoed on a smaller scale all around the second floor. A life-sized sculpture was in one of the archway recesses, illuminated by small floodlights. It wouldn't have surprised her to see a tour group appear in the wake of a guide, except that she could feel the emptiness of the vast house almost echoing around them.

Julien didn't say anything until they reached the top of the stairs. Behind them they now had a birds'-eye view of the impressive foyer. Directly in front of them was a massive painting in an ornate gilt frame that looked as if it was by some famous artist. A scene of overdressed people with heavy-looking wigs and miserable expressions and cherubic children with cheeks as pink as Jacques's. On either side they were faced with the wide balcony and its choice of countless doors.

'*Incroyable...*'

'Pardon?'

He swept his hand in a gesture that took in everything around them. 'I don't understand,' he said. 'This is not a home. It's a...a...'

'Museum?'

'*Exactement.* A gallery to display wealth. How could anyone want to *live* here?'

His sister had wanted to. Was that what he couldn't understand?

'I expect Jacques's grandmother is just as wealthy?'

'It's not the money,' Julien said. 'It's the way of thinking. The...first thoughts?'

'Priorities?'

'*Oui.*'

Walking briskly, Julien was throwing open doors. Alice caught glimpses of over-furnished bedrooms with four-poster beds and heavy velvet drapes. An overly masculine one and then a very feminine one beside it. Had his sister not shared a room with her husband?

Interior doors stood open to give a glimpse of bathrooms with marble floors and golden tapware. There was a huge sitting room with luxurious cream leather seating and a television screen big enough to make it a private movie theatre.

'I just thought of something.'

'What?'

'The grandmother. She won't be allowed to come to the house, will she?'

'No...' Julien turned his head as they walked further down the gallery that ran parallel with the front of the house.

'Or to take Jack away. Not for...for ages. A couple of weeks perhaps. Will that give you enough time?'

'I don't know if time will be enough.'

'It couldn't hurt, though, could it? Showing that you can care for him?'

Julien was silent. He had opened another door and here it was. A room that looked like an interior designer had used to fill a brief for the perfect nursery.

The ceiling was a pale blue with fluffy white clouds and a golden sun with a smiley face. The blue blended into the top of the walls but then gave way to green canopies of trees that sheltered every farm animal you could think of. The grass they stood on was sprinkled with a rainbow of flowers. Piles of toys that Jacques was far too young to appreciate—like model racing cars that were miniature Ferraris and Maseratis—filled the corners of the room but the important things were there as well. A comfortable chair for someone who needed to feed a baby. A cot with a colourful mobile hanging above it and a row of teddy bears at the foot end. On the wall behind the cot huge wooden letters in primary colours spelled out the name 'JACQUES'. Each letter was intricately adorned with tiny pictures of animals and toys.

Alice went straight towards a change table that had shelves stuffed with disposable nappies and wipes and creams and gently put Jacques down on the soft, washable surface. She stroked his hair back and smiled as he opened his eyes.

'You were loved, little one, weren't you? What a beautiful room they made for you.'

Julien said nothing. He was still opening doors.

'There's a small kitchen,' he reported. 'And a bathroom. And a bedroom that must be for the nanny.'

'Are there bottles and things in the kitchen? Tins of milk formula?'

'There's a lot of things.' Julien's voice faded as he moved back. 'Yes…bottles and cleaning things. A microwave oven.' She could hear a cupboard door closing. 'Many tins. It looks like the baby section of a supermarket.'

A rubbish bin with a tightly fitting lid was available for the soiled nappy and wipes, and by the time Julien had finished exploring and arranging items that might be useful on the bench Alice had given Jacques a quick sponge bath and fastened a clean nappy in place. Now he was sucking on his fist and grizzling.

'I think he's hungry. I'll make up some formula.'

'Do you know how?'

'I've seen it done. I don't work with the very young children at our nursery school very often but our staff kitchen is shared by everyone. There'll be instructions on the tin if I forget.'

'In French,' Julien reminded her.

'Oh…of course. Could you translate for me?'

'Of course.'

'Could you hold him? I'll need two hands.'

'Why don't you hold him and tell me what to do? I'm used to being in kitchens. I can follow a recipe.' He took off his black jacket and rolled up the sleeves of his black shirt.

He was avoiding contact again but Alice let it go. Something had changed since they'd entered the nursery. The cold, empty feeling of this vast house had been left behind in favour of these bright colours and attention to detail—the evidence that this little person had been wanted and loved. Some of the weirdness and tension had gone.

Julien actually looked a lot happier in this small kitchen as he found the measuring spoons and distilled water and made up the bottle of formula. Clearly, he could have easily done it by himself by following the instructions but Alice found herself enjoying watching. He had clever hands and his movements were deft and confident. He only frowned when he took the bottle from the microwave.

'I haven't found a thermometer. How can we check the temperature?'

'Sprinkle a few drops on the inside of your wrist. It shouldn't feel hot.'

Jacques's whimpers became a demanding cry as he spotted the bottle and Alice hurried towards the chair near the cot. She could see Julien wiping down the bench in the kitchenette as she settled back to feed the baby and it struck her as odd that a rock god could be so domesticated.

Nice odd, though.

The bench was as spotless as possible and all the kitchen items were back in place. There was no reason for him to stay here any longer.

Except...he didn't want to leave.

As he turned away from the bench he could see Alice sitting in the chair, feeding the baby. The light in the room was fading rapidly and she'd turned on the nearby lamp.

His sister had never had the chance to sit like that—her head bent and one hand supporting the end of the bottle. Had she dreamed of what it might be like to have a baby staring back at you like that, with a tiny hand that also seemed to be holding the bottle?

Memories raced even further back as he leaned a shoulder against the kitchen door. Had Colette felt the kind of love for this infant before he was born that their mother had given the two of them once, so long ago? The kind of love that had made him protect his little sister against so many odds? Had those dreams and that love stirred these poignant feelings of loss and regret but also shone a light of hope into a dark space?

The hope that came from a fresh beginning. A chance to start again and make things right this time.

He could feel that hope himself and it was like

nothing he'd ever felt. But, then, he'd never been so emotionally exhausted. So beset with problems that were coming at him from so many directions. This was a brief moment when he could actually avoid thinking about any of those problems.

Or maybe not. The buzz of the phone in his pocket came a split second before the ringtone.

He moved to the windows as he answered the call. It was dark outside now but he could see the glow of light from the street beyond the gates. A car that was waiting for permission to enter.

He raised a hand in an apologetic gesture towards Alice as he headed for the door and she smiled her understanding as she nodded.

A dreamy kind of smile, he noticed only after he'd left the room. Did holding babies automatically have that kind of effect on women? Maybe it had something to do with the soft glow of light bathing the chair and making Alice's hair glow like the last embers of a fire. Or how dark her eyes were in that pale face. Or simply how tender that smile had been.

Whatever it was, it had changed Julien's perspective. She didn't need to enhance or bleach her hair colour or have some stylish cut. She had no need of the layers of make-up he thought any attractive woman relied on. Alice McMillan wasn't simply pretty, as he'd first thought.

She was stunning.

The realisation came on top of that strange feeling he'd got watching her with the baby. It was still sucking him back in time as he hurried downstairs. Sending him over ground so old it felt new again.

How much of all this was his own fault?

If he only spent more time with Colette, she wouldn't have been able to hang out with her friends so much, using movies and trashy magazines to sculpt her view of a perfect life where only money was needed to put the world right and give her everything she could possibly want. He'd fed that belief himself, in fact, by working so hard and being so careful of every euro he earned.

If he'd been more of a father figure, perhaps

she wouldn't have fallen for a man who'd been thirty years older than her.

The regret was so intense it was painful but somehow, in the back of his mind, he could still sense that smile Alice had given him. Could still feel the softness of that moment of hope.

Crazy, considering everything that had happened today. Was it any wonder his thoughts were so scrambled? He was heading out to the gates to meet the DNA expert—a bizarre twist to this dreadful day that he could never have imagined. The quarantine on top of that was like a bad joke.

But Julien wasn't laughing.

What was that saying? You had to laugh or you would cry?

He couldn't do that either.

He seemed to have forgotten how.

Minutes ticked by in the quiet nursery.

Jacques had finished his bottle of milk and Alice lifted him to her shoulder and began to rub his back. He nestled against her and she could feel his breath on her neck. The misery of his day had caught up with him and now that he was clean and fed, she could feel the heaviness of an infant slipping into deep slumber.

His body didn't feel unnaturally hot now but that was probably because of the paracetamol the doctor had administered. He would need some more during the night. His warmth was comforting and Alice loved the tiny snuffling sounds he was making. She had probably been sitting here cuddling him for too long, though. He needed his own bed and a good sleep to help him on his journey to recovery.

He made no protest as Alice laid him gently into his cot. She pulled the blanket back and tucked him in with only a sheet for cover. She would check again soon to make sure he was neither too warm nor cold. There was a lump down the side of the cot and when she pulled it out, Alice found it was an old toy. A faded rabbit that looked as if it had been knitted out of brown fabric.

A very different toy from all the bright new

offerings in the room so it had to be special in some way. She tucked it in beside Jacques, with just the head and ears above the sheet.

She needed to find somewhere to sleep herself before too long—in the nanny's room perhaps. Not that sleep would come easily if she didn't get something to eat. Lunch seemed a very long time ago now and her stomach was rumbling.

And where was Julien? It had to be more than half an hour ago that he'd received that phone call and vanished but she couldn't go looking for him. The house was far too big to hear a baby crying. She certainly couldn't hear any sounds coming from downstairs. It was too quiet, in fact. Reaching up, Alice wound the handle on the mobile above the cot. The carousel of bright toys began turning slowly to the soft notes of 'Brahms's Lullaby'.

It was then that she noticed the baby monitor handset on the shelf beside the cot, tucked in between a soft toy unicorn and a dragon. She turned it on and suddenly an image of Jacques appeared on the screen above a speaker grill.

Startled, Alice looked around and finally spotted the camera mounted on the wall at the end of the cot.

She'd heard parents discussing baby cams but had never seen one in action. This was perfect. She could go in search of something to eat and not only hear if Jacques woke up, she'd be able to see him. A quick visit to the nursery bathroom to freshen up and Alice was ready. Eager even.

It was only because she was alone in a strange house, she told herself. Any adult company would do. It wasn't that she wanted to see Julien again.

So why did her heart do a funny double beat thing when she tiptoed out onto the gallery and saw the tall, dark figure coming towards *her*?

Julien was carrying something.

'I have the testing kit,' he told her. 'We couldn't allow the DNA expert to come into the house but he's given me very detailed instructions on how to take the test. He's waiting outside the gate to collect it when we finish. I've already found the items that might be sufficient from…André.'

The hesitation was tiny but spoke volumes.

How much did you have to hate a person to make it difficult to even say his name?

And the reminder of why she had come here in the first place had wiped out that warm glow that cuddling a sleepy baby had given Alice. It had certainly eliminated any inexplicable excitement that seeing Julien had provoked. This was business. A necessary step that might give him permission to send her packing. How could she have forgotten how unwelcome her arrival had been? That she might only have a single night to clasp that hope of family to her heart?

'Fine.' Her voice was tight. 'Tell me what to do.'

'No. I have to do it. I'm the one who has been briefed.' Julien's tone was brisk. 'Come with me. We need a place with good light.'

He took her to one of the bedrooms that they had opened a door on during their first exploration of this second floor. The feminine one. They went through the bedroom into the en suite bathroom, which was clinically bright once all the lights had been snapped on.

Alice put the monitor handset on the marble top of the vanity unit.

'What's that?'

'A monitor. So I can hear when Jack wakes up. See?' Alice touched the screen and the image of Jacques's face appeared. Like all babies, he looked like an angel with that cupid's bow of a mouth relaxed in sleep. The sweet sound of the lullaby still playing made the picture all the more adorable.

'Jacques.' Julien corrected her pronunciation, emphasising the soft 'J' as he busied himself pulling items from the bag he was carrying.

'We do two tests. One is a back-up in case there isn't enough DNA in the first sample.' He placed two small, plastic vials on the vanity top. Then he took a long packet and peeled open the end to reveal a stick that he took hold of carefully.

'I must not touch the swab or I might contaminate it.' He stepped closer to Alice. 'Open your mouth, please.'

Suddenly, this was excruciatingly embarrassing. She had a strange, *extremely* good-looking man standing close enough to kiss her and he'd asked her to open her mouth. Alice had to close her eyes as she complied. She could feel the prickle of heat rising rapidly from in front of her neck to her face. Please, let this be over quickly, she begged silently.

'I have to scrape the inside of your cheek for forty-five to sixty seconds,' Julien told her. 'The pressure will be firm. I have to collect cheek cells, not your saliva.'

Oh… God… How long could sixty seconds feel like?

For ever, that was how long. The swab on the end of the stick was like a toothbrush made of firm cotton balls. She could feel it moving up and down on the inside of her cheek. She could feel Julien's hand so close to her face she was sure that her lips were registering the warmth of his skin.

It was doing something very odd to parts of her body that had nothing to do with this test. Quite apart from the blush, her heart was hammering and there were butterflies dancing deep down in her belly.

'Bien...' The swab was finally removed from her mouth and then Julien concentrated on opening the plastic vial and inserting the swab into the liquid it contained. Then he pressed a spike on the end of the stick that released the swab and allowed him to screw back the lid of the vial. She watched his face in the mirror as he focused on his task. His hair wasn't as smooth as it had been. A thin tress had escaped the ponytail and flopped forward.

The butterflies, which had almost stopped dancing when the procedure had finished, started beating a new tattoo as Alice failed to head off a totally ridiculous desire to reach out and smooth that wayward tress back into place.

It was unfortunate that Julien chose that moment to raise his gaze and caught her looking at him in the mirror. For a heartbeat, time stopped as they stared at each other in the mirror. The bright lighting made it so easy to see the way his eyes darkened. Had he guessed that Alice was thinking about touching him? Had the urge suddenly become contagious?

Hurriedly, she dropped her gaze and Julien cleared his throat at exactly the same moment.

'One more,' he said. 'And then we're done.'

This time, Alice stood like a statue while her other cheek was scraped and she didn't risk any glance towards the mirror as he dealt with the swab and then sealed both vials into a plastic specimen bag.

There was a moment's silence when he'd finished and Alice almost wished to hear a baby's cry from the monitor, which would give her an excuse to flee. Was Julien looking into the mirror again? Looking at *her* as she avoided looking at *him*?

It was still heavy in the air—that moment when they hadn't been able to look away from each other's reflections. Something had happened. Some nameless, unexpected, *unwanted*…thing.

'You need to sign this consent form. Here—I have a pen.'

He handed her the pen and as he did so his hand brushed hers.

No more than a whisper of a touch but it felt like her skin had been burned.

Alice's signature had never been quite this shaky before. She folded the paper and handed it back and this time she looked up at Julien.

There was no getting away from it. Now that it had happened, this thing couldn't be taken back. Even if she didn't look, she had been sure it was still there.

And looking had just confirmed it.

CHAPTER FIVE

WHAT, IN GOD'S NAME, had just happened there?

The last few days—ever since he'd heard about André's accident—had made Julien feel as if his world was tipping on its axis, and the events of today had already made the angle a lot steeper. At the precise moment he'd met Alice's gaze in the mirror for the second time, it had felt like he'd just fallen off the edge of it.

Those *eyes*...

Who was this woman? This flame-haired Scottish pixie who'd not only crossed his path so unexpectedly, she was now an integral part of his life being brought to a crashing halt.

And...it felt...*good*?

Who knew where that moment could have gone if her stomach hadn't suddenly rumbled too loudly to be ignored—a sound that made Alice blush scarlet.

'Oh…pardon *me*.'

The way the colour flooded her face was fascinating but Julien wasn't going to make things any more weird by staring. And how was it that he'd only just noticed how intimate a space a bathroom was?

'You're hungry.' He turned on his heel as he made the redundant announcement. 'Come…I will get these delivered to the gate and then we'll find out what the kitchen has to offer.'

He kept a step or two ahead of Alice as he led the way downstairs but he was acutely aware that she was following. Was she still blushing? He'd never met a woman who blushed. Or whose stomach rumbled like a train, for that matter. Julien's lips twitched at the thought of either of those occurrences happening with any of the sophisticated, perfectly groomed women who'd always been available and more than willing to share his companionship and his bed.

This foreign pixie was certainly very different.

Nice different. It made him think of times with Colette before she'd learned to be sophisticated.

Not that it was unusual to remember things from the past—especially in the last few months when the grief had had to be endured, but this was the first time it could bring even an inward smile. When something poignant but sweet was stronger than any associated pain.

He sent the samples out with the security guard and remembered to issue instructions that no one else was to come through the gates, no matter how certain they were about their rights. Madame Laurent could be referred to his solicitor for more information. Or her own, for that matter. Both those men were now probably confined to their own homes and less than happy about it but what could they do?

What could any of them do about it?

At least he could do the thing that was guaranteed to relieve stress.

He could cook.

'Oh, my goodness...' Alice stopped in the doorway to the kitchen. 'This looks like a commercial kitchen. You could cook enough to feed an army in here. Or run a restaurant.'

And it was clean, Julien noted with satisfaction, eyeing the expanse of stainless-steel benches.

'There's no fridge!' Alice exclaimed. 'How strange…'

'There'll be a cold room, I expect. And a pantry. You're right…this has been set up as a commercial kitchen. Look…' Julien walked past the hobs and ovens and through an arched doorway into a scullery. Sure enough, there was a pantry and if he'd thought the cupboard in the nursery had looked like a section of a supermarket, it was nothing on what was stocked in here. The cold room was just as well stocked.

'Oh…' Alice's eyes were round with surprise. 'Look at all that *cheese*…' She grinned at Julien. 'I *love* cheese…'

It was the first time he'd seen her really smile and he got that strange falling sensation all over again. He found himself smiling back because he couldn't help it.

'Take some out,' he told her. 'See if you can

find some bread and olives. There'll be a wine cellar somewhere but we'll make do with what's cold. Here…take this one. I'll see what I can find to cook with.'

'But it's champagne…*French* champagne.'

Julien's lips twitched again. 'I wasn't aware there was any other kind.'

'But…'

'Mmm?' Julien was gathering some ingredients. Minced beef and garlic and chilli. Greens and parmesan cheese. He needed something quick and easy. Pasta and salad should be perfect. Reaching for a bottle of balsamic vinegar, he became aware of the silence behind him. He turned to find Alice looking bewildered. He raised his eyebrows.

'Champagne is for celebrating something,' she said quietly.

Julien stopped thinking about food. 'Maybe we can find something to celebrate, then.'

Her eyes widened. 'Like what?'

Oh, no… How insensitive was it to suggest that she should be celebrating something when she'd just found out that her probable father was deceased? He had to think fast as he moved past her to drop his armload on a bench.

'You may have discovered a brother,' he suggested. 'And…and have you ever been to France before?'

'No…never…'

'*Donc*… There you go. That is definitely worth celebrating.'

'And what about you? What have you got to celebrate?'

'Ah…' Julien stared down at his ingredients without seeing them. Nothing. He was revisiting the grief from losing his sister. He had a major problem in what to do about the show that filming was due to start on within days. He probably had to face a court case over custody of his nephew that was highly likely to get very nasty.

No. Nothing to celebrate there.

He looked up, ready to admit defeat and agree that champagne might not be the most appropriate thing to drink.

And then he got caught by those eyes again.

What was it that he could see?

Hope?

Optimism?

A belief in fairy-tales, even?

Something shifted in his chest and he found himself saying something he hadn't thought of until now.

'I got to hold my sister's baby for the first time today.' The words came out as little more than a whisper and he was embarrassed that he was showing so much emotion in front of a stranger. He cleared his throat. 'And I have a reprieve from having to deal with Madame Laurent.' He offered a crooked smile. 'That is absolutely worth celebrating, *n'est-ce pas*?'

She'd made him smile.

Sort of. One of those oddly endearing lopsided ones like he'd given her when he had asked for her help with Jacques, but it felt like a victory because there was something very sombre about Julien's face—especially his eyes—and she got the impression that he didn't smile, let alone laugh, very often.

She sat at the big central table in this enormous kitchen, with the baby monitor in one hand and a glass of champagne in the other, and watched Julien cook.

The champagne was astonishingly delicious and Julien…well, he was just as astonishing. The way he chopped vegetables with a speed that made her blink and then scooped them up to drop them into a food processor as if it was the easiest thing in the world to do without making a mess. He got two frying pans going on gas flames on the hobs and in one of them he was adding things to minced beef like mustard and balsamic vinegar and a huge handful of herbs that had also been chopped with lightning efficiency. The smell was starting to make Alice feel very, very hungry and the champagne on her empty stomach was making her head spin a little. She watched as Julien tossed the contents of the pan, which mixed the contents more efficiently than a wooden spoon, which would have been her choice of implement.

'You really know your way around a kitchen, don't you?'

A snort that could have been laughter came from Julien. 'I should hope so. I've been working in them for twenty years now.'

'Twenty years? You don't look old enough to have been working that long.'

'I'm thirty-five.'

'You started working when you were fifteen? After school?'

'No.' Julien carelessly sprinkled a handful of sea salt flakes into a pot of boiling water and then tipped a packet of pasta in. 'I had to drop out of school.'

'Why?' Alice wouldn't normally ask such personal questions of someone she had only just met but the champagne was making her reckless.

'My mother died. I had to get my sister away from our stepfather and I had to support her. The only job I could get was washing dishes in a restaurant. Sometimes I was given other jobs to help the chefs and…and I was good at it.' He lifted his glass in a toast. 'And so I learned to cook.'

He'd taken off his tie and unbuttoned the top of his shirt before he'd started work in the kitchen and his sleeves were pushed up as far as they could go. The escaping tress of his hair had been joined by a couple more and his cheeks were pink from the heat of the stove. He looked dishevelled. And…as delicious as the smell of whatever he was cooking. Alice could only begin to imagine how many fans he must have.

'And you're a musician as well…'

'*Pardon? Je ne comprends pas…*'

The puzzlement on his face made the meaning of his words clear.

'The show you were talking about? The film crews? I thought…you must be a singer. In a band.'

He was looking at her as if she'd lost her mind. 'It's a show for television. Food television.'

Alice's jaw dropped. 'Food television? You're a…*chef*?' Images of a rock star were being blown apart. No wonder the doctor's wife was such a fan. Maybe the media waiting outside the gates had nothing to do with how famous her father had been.

'*Exactement*. The Christmas show I was talking about? It is for a morning television show on Christmas Eve. I am demonstrating a traditional English Christmas dinner to compare with another chef who is doing the French one.' Julien drained his glass of champagne and came over to the table to refill both their glasses. 'The actual cooking will be pre-recorded but I will be a guest on the live show to talk about it on the day. If my test doesn't confirm my immunity so that I can leave this house, it will be a mess that will be very difficult to deal with. A lot of people will be extremely annoyed.'

As if in sympathy with the statement, a whimper came through the monitor. It was a startling reminder of the responsibility they both had to Jacques and for a long moment they both stared at the screen of the handset but, with another tired-sounding cry, the baby settled back into sleep.

Julien sank into the chair opposite Alice, his

gaze still focused on the screen, his brow furrowed. 'What is that?'

'What?'

'In the bed with him? That...'

'Oh...it's a toy. A rabbit. I thought it must be special because it looks very old.'

The way Julien's throat moved suggested that he was having trouble swallowing.

'It's *le lapin brun*... It was Colette's special toy when she was tiny. I...didn't know she had kept it.' His voice cracked. 'She must have put it in the nursery before he was born because...I don't think she ever saw him after he was born...'

Tears sprang to Alice's eyes. 'That's so sad...' Then she shook her head slowly, in disbelief. 'Such a tragedy... Was...was she very sick?'

'*Non*. She had come to see me only the week before. The first time I had seen her in over a year and she had never looked so well. She was so excited about the baby. It made her want to reconnect with her own family, she said. It made her remember...'

He had closed his eyes and that gave Alice permission to let her gaze linger on his face as he seemingly became lost in his own thoughts.

Dear Lord, even when you couldn't see those astonishing eyes, he was a beautiful man with those strong features and such a sensitive-looking mouth. Eyelashes that caught your attention because they were a little longer than you'd expect on a man—like his hair.

This was no time to ask what had caused such a rift between these siblings. Whatever it had been, it sounded like they'd been ready to forgive and forget. 'What did she remember?' Alice asked softly to break the silence.

'That her first memories were of how I'd looked after her. How important I'd been in her life for ever. That she didn't want to lose that and that, maybe, this baby could help bring us back together. And I thought she was right. She texted me when she went into the hospital and so I went to visit and…and I saw her die…'

'Oh, my God… *No*…' It was instinctive to reach out to touch him. To cover his hand with her own.

His eyes were open again and the shock of his words cut even deeper as she saw unshed tears making them glisten.

'They said it was an *embolie*. I don't know the word for it in English…'

'An embolism?'

'*Probablement*.' Julien shook off the translation as unimportant. 'Something to do with the water around the baby and it gave her an attack of the heart and… *Il ne pouvait rien faire*… They tried. I *saw* how hard they try…'

That his English was fractured only made this more heart-breaking. Alice could feel Julien's distress so deeply that, unlike him, she couldn't stop tears escaping, but he didn't need her reaction to make the memories worse. He needed something very different.

Comfort.

With a huge effort Alice banished her tears and steadied her voice. She squeezed Julien's hand as she spoke.

'I love it that Jacques has the rabbit,' she said softly, paying careful attention to pronouncing the name correctly. 'One day you'll be able to tell him how special it is. And how much his mother must have loved him to give it to him.'

The glance she received was almost bewildered. And then Julien gave his head a tiny shake as if he was sending those memories back where they belonged. In the past. He stood up, sliding his hand from beneath Alice's with no acknowledgment that she had touched him, and her fingers curled as she pulled her hand back.

She could only see his back now.

'Let's eat. My penne ragout will be ready.'

He was too tired to feel particularly hungry.

Or perhaps his brain was too occupied with other things to notice he was only picking at his food.

The words Alice had spoken were turning slowly, a new ingredient that was going to simmer in his head, along with everything else that had happened today, like a kind of emotional ragout.

Memories associated with the brown rabbit

were strong enough to throw the mix off balance. The sight of it shocking enough to make him talk to someone about that terrible day for the first time.

Maybe it was easier to be open with a stranger?

Except that it hadn't felt like he'd been with a stranger. Alice was different. She was real. And she cared. That human touch of comfort had almost left a brand on his skin that he could still feel.

He hadn't seen that toy for so many years he had forgotten how important *le lapin brun* had been. Colette would not go to sleep without it. And if he'd taken her to hide—under a bed perhaps—to escape one of their stepfather's drunken rages, then brown bunny made it so much more bearable. Little Colette would cuddle the toy. And he would cuddle Colette.

And now Jacques was sleeping with it and Alice had found something good about that. Something to celebrate…

But that was confusing the flavour he'd been so sure was the right one for whatever recipe his head and heart were inventing—the cocktail of grief and resentment and even hatred. He could imagine Colette putting the toy into the bed she had prepared for her baby and gifting him the thing that had brought her such comfort, but for him to have it suggested that André had known of the toy's significance and he'd wanted his son to have something precious that had belonged to his mother...

Because he'd cared?

Because he'd loved Colette that much?

If that was true, then he himself had been wrong in trying to stop the marriage by persuading Colette what a terrible mistake she was making. It would make those strained months of him not being welcome in his sister's home—after the wedding he'd refused to attend—a stupid, wasted opportunity. And the sworn hatred between the two men wouldn't have overridden almost everything else at Colette's funeral.

He knew he had failed her but maybe it was in a different way than he'd thought.

'This is amazing...' Alice's words broke the

increasingly negative spiral of his thoughts. 'It's the best pasta I have ever eaten. It's…it's *magnifique*…'

Her passable attempt at a French word made Julien tilt his head in acknowledgement of both her effort and the compliment. It made him look up and catch her gaze and it seemed like every time that happened it became more familiar and the hit of whatever it was that the eye contact gave him became more powerful.

He couldn't identify what it was but there was no getting away from the knowledge that it warmed something deep inside his chest. It was something as real as the comforting touch she had given him. Maybe he hadn't known how precious little of anything that real there was in his life.

'*Merci beaucoup*. I am delighted that you like it.'

Suddenly Julien felt hungry himself. Really hungry. He loaded up forkful of the pasta coated in the spicy sauce and could taste it properly now. Yes, that balsamic vinegar had added a perfect, balancing note to the sweetness of the tomatoes and the bite of chilli.

A small thing in the grand scheme of things but it was often the small things that could be unexpectedly important, wasn't it?

Like an old, battered toy…

By the time Alice had finished eating her delicious meal it was obvious that she could barely keep her eyes open.

'Dessert?' Julien offered. 'Some coffee, perhaps?'

'No, thank you. I…I should go and check on Jacques and then I think I need some sleep myself. I thought I would use the nanny's bed, if that's all right? That way I'll be close when he wakes. He may need a night feed and I'm sure he'll need some more paracetamol before morning.'

Morning. The start of a new day and who knew what new problems might present themselves? Julien rubbed his temples. He had more than enough to deal with now. Too much. Top of that list would be to call a teleconference and try to organise a way to manage the fallout if he couldn't film the Christmas show. He had tried to contact the head of his production team as soon as the doctor had dropped the quarantine bombshell but he hadn't got through. And then he'd been completely distracted, hadn't he—at first by the appalling thought of Alice having to stay in the house and then by the emotional rollercoaster that had started the moment he'd held his sister's child in his arms for the first time ever.

It was all too much. He needed some time out and maybe it wasn't too late to try and make the first of those calls tonight. He pulled his phone from his pocket and was already scrolling his contacts list as he spoke.

'I'll use one of the rooms near the nursery,' he told Alice. 'You can call if you need help with anything.'

'Don't worry…I'm sure I can cope.' There was a moment's silence and he knew Alice was looking at him, waiting for him to look up, but he resisted the urge. Enough was enough. If that peculiar sensation he got when he met her eyes kept happening, he might have to try and identify it so that he would know how to deal with it. And he had the funny feeling that giving it a name might only open a whole new can of worms.

He knew she had gone by more than the sound of her boots on the flagged floor of the kitchen.

Her departure also left the room feeling disturbingly empty.

CHAPTER SIX

THE MESSAGE HAD been crystal clear.

It felt like they'd been so close in those moments when Alice had been holding Julien's hand as he'd told her about the tragedy of his sister's death but he hadn't even looked at her when she'd excused herself to check on Jacques, and whatever barrier he'd put up around himself, having pushed her away, was still firmly in place the next morning.

He barely came near the nursery for the whole morning, other than to bring her a tray of coffee and some amazingly melt-in-the-mouth croissants, still warm from the oven, at seven a.m. At nine a.m., with a phone in his hand, he came briefly to the door to ask if Jacques was any worse and if she needed the doctor to visit today. He vanished as soon as she shook her head.

Being abandoned upstairs with an unwell baby should have felt lonely. Scary even, but the time was passing quickly and, for such a huge house with only one other adult in it, it felt surprisingly busy.

Phones were ringing at frequent intervals and delivery vans began arriving from mid-morning. From the nursery windows Alice could see them coming up the driveway, and if she was near the door to this suite of rooms she could hear Julien talking downstairs or faint clattering sounds from the direction of the kitchens.

Would he deliver another tray for her lunch? And then dinner after a whole afternoon alone with Jacques? By one p.m. Alice felt like she'd been sent to Coventry—as punishment perhaps for engaging in a conversation that had become too personal. She didn't even try and ignore her rebellious streak this time. As soon as Jacques was down for a sleep after a lunchtime feed, she took the baby cam monitor and marched downstairs.

Her determined stride faltered at the bottom of

the stairs. There were boxes littering the foyer. A suitcase. And...

'Good *grief...*'

Julien appeared from the kitchen, wiping his hands on a dish towel.

'*C'est horrible, n'est pas*?'

'*Horrible.*' Alice tried to repeat the word. 'It's a...a *monster*.'

A monster bright blue teddy bear that was in the corner beside the door.

'It is a gift from Madame Laurent. It has a tag that says, "For my beloved grandson".'

Alice let out an incredulous huff. 'It's five times the size of her grandson. It would probably terrify him.'

'That is why I have left it down here.'

'And the suitcase?'

'Some clothing and other things I needed. I can arrange for some to be brought for you?'

'I'll manage. I have a spare shirt and...' a blush threatened as she stopped herself mentioning underwear '...things. I'm fine. I just came down for...' *Some company.* 'For something to eat.'

'Come.' Julien's hand wave encompassed the boxes. 'I have had many things delivered, including some work that needed extra food.'

Alice followed him into the kitchen. There were pots simmering on the stove and the table was covered with sheets of paper, most of which had glossy photographs along with the text.

'Is that a recipe book?'

'They are the—how do you say it—proofing pages?' Julien began scooping them into a heap. 'There is a deadline and I want to check some of the recipes by cooking them again. What would you like for your lunch? A mushroom risotto perhaps? Or chicken Dijon?'

Alice chose the risotto. He presented it to her on a tray but Alice didn't want to leave the room, even if he was busy working. She sat at the table and watched him. She hadn't intended interrupting him any further but she only took a few mouthfuls before her good intentions evaporated.

'How do I say "I love it" in French?'

The smile was the kind of lopsided one he'd given her more than once now. Maybe that was the only way Julien smiled. It meant something, though, because he stopped what he was doing and came to sit opposite her.

'*Je l'aime.*'

Alice repeated the phrase. 'And if I want to say "I *don't* like it"?'

'*Je ne l'aime pas.*' Julien frowned. 'You *don't* like the risotto?'

She grinned. 'No. *Je l'aime.* A lot.'

'*Beaucoup.*' He listened to her repetition. 'You have a good accent,' he told her.

The praise was unexpected and Alice felt suddenly shy. 'I think I'd like to learn French,' she admitted. 'I was never allowed to take it at school and I haven't really listened to it properly before but…it's beautiful. Like music.'

'It is a beautiful language.' Julien gave her a curious look. 'Why were you not allowed to learn at school?'

Alice had to look away. 'Because of who my father was, I imagine. My mother never talked about it but my grandmother hated anything French.'

Julien let her eat in silence for a minute. 'Perhaps your mother hated André Laurent, too, after the way he treated her.'

'I don't think so. If she had, she might have found someone else she could fall in love with and she never did. I don't think she even tried.'

'Perhaps your village was too small.'

'It was small but Mum trained to be a nurse after I was born and she met a lot of people through her work.'

'And she had you to care for.'

'Yes.' Alice glanced at the monitor as she ate another mouthful of the delicious risotto. 'I can imagine loving my child so much that I would be wary of anything that might change my life.' Then she laid down her fork and sighed 'Or maybe her heart had just been broken too badly. I know a lot of people think it's nonsense but— for some—I think there really is only "the one".'

Julien was giving her another one of those odd, unreadable looks. 'And you? Are you one of the "some"?'

Again, Alice had to look away. How silly was

it that her heart had started thumping so loudly she was afraid he might hear it? But she nodded slowly.

'Yes. I think I'm one of those people.'

Julien's chair scraped as he pushed it back abruptly. 'I hope you find this "one", then, Alice.'

She took her plate over to the sink beside which he was working again. 'Sometimes that's not enough,' she told him. 'He will have to find me, too.'

It was the sound of the baby crying early the next morning that woke Julien.

It was still crying as he pulled on his jeans. A sharp cry that was suddenly alarming.

Still too sleepy to think clearly, he threw open his door and ran to the nursery. Jacques was in his cot. Alice was nowhere to be seen.

'Alice?'

There was no answer. The kitchenette was deserted and there was no sound of running water from the bathroom.

The noise level was still increasing. Julien

walked to the cot and stood looking down at his nephew. He had no idea what he should do. Surely Alice would come through the door and rescue him?

Jacques was sobbing. His little fists were waving in the air and his face was bright red.

'Shh...' Julien said. *Alice vient bientôt. Tout est okay...'*

Except it wasn't okay. Jacques let out a piercing shriek and he couldn't stand there and do nothing. Reaching into the cot, he picked up the baby and then held it against his chest. A still-bare chest, he realised belatedly that now had a warm little head resting on it as he rocked the baby and tried to make soothing noises into the miniature ear.

Miraculously, it seemed to be working. The shrieking lessened to a wail and then to a series of hiccupping sobs. And then Jacques started rubbing his nose on Julien's chest and the movement got slower and slower and then stopped. Julien noticed two things. That Jacques seemed to have gone back to sleep and that one tiny fist was locked around his thumb.

No. Make that three things. He had picked up this distressed baby and had been able to comfort him. He felt proud of himself. And then he felt...something much deeper. This tiny person was trusting him enough to fall asleep in his arms. To protect him from any evil that might be present in the unknown world around them. Such absolute trust from a being so completely vulnerable was doing something peculiar to his heart because it felt so full it could burst.

He should go and find Alice and hand over the care of the baby because this was precisely what he had been afraid of. Feeling the kind of bond that would inevitably lead to heartache, no matter how this situation got resolved.

He had known it would only make it harder to hold his sister's baby and Alice couldn't be far away so he could escape.

He just didn't want to move quite yet.

Alice had been running up the stairs as she'd heard that alarming shriek over the monitor.

She'd gone down to the kitchen to find something for her breakfast because Julien wasn't awake yet and she'd stupidly left the monitor there to go and find a downstairs bathroom. How long had he been crying like that?

She wasn't even halfway up the stairs when the increased force of the baby's cries made her check the screen of her monitor and that was when she saw that Jacques wasn't alone.

Julien was standing beside the cot. Half-dressed. Good grief, he hadn't even fastened the button of his jeans and she could see the white fabric of his underwear exposed. As for the rest of him…oh, my… A torso and arms with sculpted muscle that begged to be traced with gentle hands. A face that was so twisted with indecision that a sympathetic smile tugged at Alice's lips and she wanted to hug even more than stroke this man.

She should keep going and rescue him because he clearly had no idea what to do about Jacques but Alice's steps involuntarily came to a halt. She was holding her breath when she saw Julien reach into the cot and then she had to swallow past a huge lump in her throat as she saw him cradle the baby against his bare chest and start rocking him.

It was an image that would have melted any woman's heart but it was bigger than that for Alice because it got added to her memory of whatever had happened between them that had been reflected in the bathroom mirror and had since been banished.

He was an extraordinary man, wasn't he?

Completely out of her league, of course. A television star, for heaven's sake. Probably extremely wealthy and able to take his pick of a vast array of eager women.

What would she have to offer that could possibly interest someone like Julien Dubois?

Obviously nothing, which was why he had backed off so quickly. Alice started walking again. She took a deep breath and tried to shove her thoughts somewhere that wouldn't show on her face by the time she got to the nursery. If there had been a 'thing' and it hadn't been simply her imagination, then Julien had banished it and she needed to follow suit unless she wanted to totally humiliate herself.

The 'thing'—along with that heart-stealing sight of him holding Jacques—had to be jammed into a mental jar like the ones that Julien brought out from the pantry when he was cooking. Big, square glass jars with metal lids that held things like caster sugar or salt. The thing needed to be trapped and the lid tightly screwed into place. The jar couldn't be opened and the thing couldn't be allowed to grow because that might shatter the glass and possibly be as catastrophic as the way the glass on her father's portrait had shattered when Julien had hurled the paperweight at it.

So Alice wasn't even going to *think* about the muscles on that bare chest and arms. Or those unfastened jeans…

She would keep her gaze firmly on the baby when she entered the room. She would keep out of Julien's way as much as possible and when they were together she would stick to something completely safe—like the basic French lessons he had started giving her over dinner last night.

It should work.

It *had* to work.

CHAPTER SEVEN

THE PHONE RANG at exactly nine o'clock in the morning.

The way it had for three mornings now.

'Tell him that the rash is fading on his face,' Alice called in response to Julien's query. 'It certainly hasn't spread any further down his body and his temperature is normal quite a lot of the time.'

'Do you want the doctor to visit today?'

Alice shook her head, adjusting the weight of the freshly changed and fed baby in her arms from her position on the gallery, looking down to the foyer that Julien was crossing as he headed for one of the landlines in the house. 'We might need some more paracetamol syrup, that's all.'

There would be no problem having it delivered, along with any other supplies Julien deemed necessary. Vans were still being admitted through the gates every day. More gifts had arrived from Madame Laurent. Nothing as awful as the giant teddy bear but none of them had got as far as the nursery—they were piling up around the blue monstrosity in the foyer, which Alice could see from the corner of her eye as she walked with Jacques around the gallery instead of going straight back to the nursery.

Maybe she wanted to hear the sound of Julien's voice as he carried on his conversation with the doctor. No sooner had it stopped than the phone rang again. A shorter conversation this time and then a much longer silence. So long that Alice decided it was time to return to the nursery, so the sound of her name being called again startled her.

'Alice?'

Elise. It still gave her a tiny flutter of butterflies in her stomach, the way Julien pronounced her name. She turned to peer down into the foyer again.

'I'm here.'

'Could you come downstairs, please?'

Alice's heart skipped a beat. Something had changed. She was used to the level of tension in this house and how serious and almost aloof Julien was but there was a note in his voice that she had never heard before and it made her feel as if she was being summoned to the headmaster's office because she had done something wrong and she was in trouble. Her heart was in her mouth by the time she got to the bottom of the stairs.

Had the blood-test results come back to prove her immunity to measles? Was she about to be sent away and the care of Jacques assigned to someone else? Or was Julien also safe and he could escape to meet the deadline of filming his Christmas show in Paris? Alice wasn't sure which scenario would be worse. She didn't want anything to change, she realised. Not just yet.

'What is it?'

'Come...' Julien led her across the foyer, not towards the grand salon, as she might have expected for a formal discussion, but into the kitchen. This was the only room that she'd spent much time in other than the nursery.

It felt like home. Despite the size and how professional this area of the house was, it didn't have the kind of museum feel the rest of the house did, with the opulent architecture and priceless antiques so carefully positioned. Julien probably felt more at home here as well, which was why he'd chosen to use it as an office as well as a test kitchen.

Not that there were any papers strewn over the table yet this morning.

'Sit down.' The invitation was terse enough to make it sound like a command but, for once, any rebellious streak on Alice's part was dormant. She sank into a chair beside the table and shifted Jacques so that he was sitting on her lap, cradled in one arm. She rested her other hand on the tabletop, ready to provide extra support quickly if it was needed. Jacques looked up at Alice and then reached out a chubby hand to grab a fistful of her hair. He was only holding it, not tugging, so Alice let it be and shifted her gaze to Julien, who had sat down at the end of the table right beside her.

This was different, too. If they ate together, he sat opposite her. This felt more intimate. More serious. Alice swallowed hard. Something bad must have happened and the news was going to be broken gently. But she was an orphan already and had no other family so what did she have to lose?

'Oh…' Alice whispered. 'The DNA results have come back, haven't they?'

'*Oui*. The call came just after I spoke with the doctor.'

The sinking feeling was so horrible that Alice had to close her eyes. 'I was wrong, wasn't I? I'm not André's daughter. Jacques is not…not my brother…'

'*Au contraire*…' The touch of Julien's hand covering hers as it rested on the table made Alice's eyes snap open. 'That is exactly the truth. You are, without doubt, the child of André Laurent. And you are Jacquot's sister.'

Alice gasped. The flood of emotion revealed

how much she had had resting on this news. There was grief there. For the father she would never know. For her mother who had lost the man she loved and then lost her life far too soon. But there was joy, too. Immeasurable joy and hope for a future she had never imagined.

She tried to smile but imminent tears made it impossible. She tried to fight them. Tried not to be so acutely aware of how her skin felt where Julien's hand was covering hers. It felt like support. Protection. And something much more visceral. Attraction mixed with both grief and hope felt remarkably like being in love, didn't it?

She couldn't go there… Couldn't even let the thought rest long enough to take a recognisable shape.

'Jacquot?' she queried, her voice choked.

Julien shrugged. 'It is a… How do say it? A pet name? Like Jamie instead of James.' He smiled at the baby, reaching out to touch his cheek gently. 'It seems you have a big sister, little Jacquot.'

Alice lost the battle with the tears. The skin on her hand was still tingling where he'd been touching it and she knew exactly what the stroke of that finger on the baby's cheek would feel like. Tender. Caring...

The tears rolled down her cheeks in big, fat droplets.

Julien glanced up and then stared at her, his brow furrowed. 'This news has made you unhappy?'

Alice shook her head. What had Julien said? '*Au contraire*,' she managed on a stifled sob. 'I... I couldn't be happier.'

A sudden tug on her hair made her look down and, as if he knew how momentous this news had been, Jacquot stared back up at the two adults.

And then it happened. His little face crinkled and then split into a grin—the first real smile Alice had seen him make.

The alchemy of her emotional turbulence found a new direction. The one it should have had all along. This was the moment that she fell completely in love with this baby.

Her *brother*...

It was a crooked little grin. Rather like the only

way she'd seen his uncle smile. Alice lifted her gaze and that might have been a mistake because it hit her again. It was so huge, this love that she had for Jacquot. Her heart could burst with the enormity but it wouldn't because some of that love was spilling out and Julien was somehow caught up in the fallout. Words formed and came out in a whisper.

'He looks like you.'

Julien met her gaze. His eyes looked bright—with unshed tears perhaps? 'I was just thinking how much he looks like Colette.'

The poignant undertone of his words made Alice want to gather him close and cuddle him the way she was cuddling Jacquot. The corners of her own mouth were still curling, as they had done in an instant response to the baby's smile, but now she could feel them wobble. She could see exactly the same struggle between happiness and sorrow hovering over the edges of Julien's lips and when she was brave enough to catch his gaze again, there it was.

The thing…

And this time it was powerful enough to feel like a punch in her gut, maybe because she recognised it for what it was. How could she not, when she'd just fallen utterly in love with her little brother?

Julien Dubois wasn't just caught up in the fallout of what she was feeling for her little brother. He was a part of what was causing this tsunami of emotion. She had somehow slipped past the warning signs that she might be in danger of falling in love with him.

For some reason she couldn't identify, there was a sense of connection in that particular look they had shared more than once now that was sucking her in and making her imagine things that couldn't possibly be true. How ridiculous was it to get a flash of thought that this man could be the person she had been searching for ever since she'd been a naïve teenager and had begun dreaming of a fairy-tale happy ending in her search for love?

They didn't even speak the same language, for heaven's sake.

They had absolutely nothing in common, other than a genetic connection to a small, orphaned child.

No wonder she hadn't been able to dismiss the memory of how that eye contact had made her feel. Or how it had been magnified by the sight of Julien standing half-naked with Jacquot in his arms. With the skin of her hand still buzzing with the memory of his touch even though it had been removed now, the air around her felt volatile. As if something could very well explode.

That imaginary glass jar perhaps?

Alice dragged her gaze free of Julien's so fast he didn't have a chance of being the first to break that contact.

They both seemed to feel the need to change the subject and they both spoke at exactly the same time.

'The doctor said...'

'I think I'd better...' Alice stopped and blinked. 'What did the doctor say?'

'That the nanny, Nicole, is showing signs of

having caught measles. She has the spots inside her cheeks. I've forgotten what he called them.'

'Koplik's spots. Oh, no… That makes this a more serious outbreak, doesn't it?'

'It would appear so. But he said that Jacques will not be contagious within another day or two and he's found a children's nurse who can come into the house and care for him. Marthe—the housekeeper—could also return as her tests have shown her to be immune.'

'*No*…' Alice surprised herself with the vehemence of her response so it was no wonder that Julien's eyebrows shot up. 'I want to look after him,' she added. 'He's…' A smile curved around her soft words. 'He's my brother.'

Julien frowned. 'It may take some time before your relationship to Jacques can be legally acknowledged. The French system of law is complicated and offices will close down for some time over the Christmas period.' His frown deepened. 'There have been repeated calls from Madame Laurent—his grandmother. She is impatient to have the child collected and taken to her home in Geneva at the earliest opportunity.'

'Have him *collected*?' Alice was shocked. 'This is her *grand*son. How could she be prepared to let total strangers come and take him away from his home? How frightening would that be? It's hard enough that he has people he doesn't know looking after him when he's sick but at least he's in a familiar place.'

'She buried her only son a few days ago. I imagine it's a taxing time for an elderly woman.'

'How old is she?'

'Given that her son was in his early sixties, I expect she's well over eighty.'

Far too old to be taking on the task of raising a baby, then. But then another thought struck Alice and it made her catch her breath.

'Good grief…do you realise that Madame Laurent is also *my* grandmother?'

Julien's chair scraped as he pushed it back. 'Of course. I hadn't thought of that.'

And it was clearly an unpleasant thought. Alice was closely related to a man he loathed. He was disappearing behind the barriers again and Alice didn't want him to go. It wasn't fair to dismiss her because of who her father or grandmother was.

'Did the doctor say anything about the blood tests? Do we know if we're cleared for immunity for measles now?'

Julien shook his head as he got to his feet. 'No. Those results are not back and although he expects it won't be any later than tomorrow, they will be too late to help. A decision about my travelling has to be made today. This morning. So the show will have to be cancelled. There is no way around it and it is a disaster.'

'You would have been allowed to travel if you had proof of immunity?'

'Yes. And I expected it would have come well before this or I would have taken the offer of being immunised again but it is too late now.'

'But other people who are immune are allowed to come into the house, aren't they? Like the nurse that we don't need?'

'It would seem so.' But Julien wasn't really listening. He had his mobile phone in his hand and was staring at the screen as he moved towards the door.

He was moving further away with every heartbeat and Alice could feel the distance growing. She should just let him go. If she couldn't see him, maybe she could clear her head—and her heart—of the nonsense that had taken root.

But her mouth opened before she could stop it.

'Why can't you film the show here?'

'*Quoi?*' Julien stopped in his tracks and turned to face Alice. 'What did you say?'

'It's just an idea…' And probably a stupid one judging by the look on Julien's face. 'This is a huge kitchen. It could be in a restaurant somewhere. How many people do you need to film a show?'

Julien shrugged. 'A skeleton crew might be only a cameraman and a sound person and someone to do the set-up and lighting. My producer perhaps.'

'What if you could find people that had proof they were immune to measles? Or if they had no chance of catching it? The kitchen has a back door, doesn't it? They wouldn't need to go into the house and I could keep Jacquot out of the way...'

The look of concentration on Julien's face was as fierce as he'd looked when he'd been cooking in the last couple of days.

'I don't know... There would be a lot of questions that need to be asked. An impossible amount of organisation to do if it was possible...but...'

But there it was.

A glimmer of hope in what had been an insurmountable problem that Julien had been putting off making a decision about because the repercussions were so huge.

Nobody in his management team would have thought of this possibility because they had no idea what the kitchens were like in the Laurent mansion but why hadn't it occurred to him?

Yet again, the little Scottish pixie had waved a magic wand.

Perhaps.

There were a dozen or more phone calls that

needed to be made and Julien didn't want to waste a single minute.

An hour of calls being made and received stretched into two hours and then three. Strings were pulled. Concessions made. Permission granted. Plans put into action.

Julien took the stairs two at a time. He burst into the nursery and Alice whirled around from where she had been bent over the cot, tucking the baby in for a sleep.

The curtains had been pulled to dim the room but a shaft of sunlight had found the gap between them and Alice turned into it, her hair glowing like a halo around her head.

Julien took a stride towards her. And then another. He caught her shoulders in her hands and bent his head to kiss her on one cheek and then the other. A perfectly ordinary greeting between French friends.

'You are an angel,' he told Alice. 'You have solved the problem of the show. *Merci, chérie. Merci beaucoup.*'

Maybe it was the way his heart had been cap-

tured by a baby smile that had made him remember his little sister with such a burst of love.
Maybe it was the way Alice's eyes were shining
with such joy at his exuberant appreciation of
having the wheels of a solution already turning.
Or maybe this had just been something that had
become inevitable ever since that first moment
of being caught by those extraordinary eyes.

Instead of leaving the kissing within those polite parameters, Julien bestowed a third kiss. Directly on Alice's lips.

A brief kiss—but not nearly brief enough because now he knew what it was he'd been trying to avoid defining. That peculiar sensation he
got when he looked into her eyes was nothing
compared to the electric shock that came from
touching her skin. Touching her hand had been
manageable. Kissing her cheeks even. But the
touch of his own lips on hers?

It was so powerful. This sense of…recognition.

Of finding something you hadn't had any idea
you were even looking for.

It couldn't be real. It had started when he'd been
in an emotionally exhausted state and right now

he was high on the relief of a massive problem being on the way to resolution.

Julien needed to remember that this woman was the daughter of the man who'd been his enemy. Who had put the knife in and twisted it in those first awful moments of trying to come to terms with his sister's death.

'You'll never see her son. My son—unless it's over my dead body...'

And she was the granddaughter of Madame Laurent—the matriarch of the family he despised who was just as determined to take his nephew out of his reach.

He was already on his way out of the room as the shock waves of his impulsive action faded into ever smaller ripples.

Julien needed to make sure he didn't touch Alice McMillan again, that was all. And that should be easy with the chaos that was about to descend on this house.

The kitchen was out of bounds for Alice as soon as the first of the convoy of trucks and vans began arriving later that day. The sound of voices and furniture scraping and even loud hammering could be heard coming from the kitchens as she wandered around upstairs with Jacquot in her arms, keeping him amused while he was awake.

Julien brought her a mug of coffee and a fresh baguette filled with ham and cheese as a late lunch.

'Filming will start very soon. There will be more than enough food for dinner later but it may be quite late. Will you be okay to wait?'

'I'll be fine. Good luck—I hope it goes well.'

Alice filled in the time easily to begin with. Jacquot was clearly feeling much better today and the smiles came more often. He even giggled when she squeaked one of his toys in his bath and Alice ignored how wet she was getting from the splashing as she leaned over to kiss him.

'You are adorable, Jacquot. I love you so much…'

It was a joy to feed him after his bath and to sing softly to him as he fell asleep and it was in the quiet moment before she put him into his cot for the night that the idea first occurred to Alice.

She could raise her little brother. She could give him a home and love him to bits, and if Julien could be persuaded that it was a good idea they could both be all the family this little boy could need. Surely the grandmother would agree that it was best? She was an old woman and it wasn't as if it was someone outside the family taking on Jacquot's care. She was his sister but she could be a mother as well.

The idea grew wings as she tucked Jacquot into his cot. Maybe Madame Laurent—and possibly Julien—would insist that Jacquot be brought up in France but Alice could manage that. She would learn this beautiful language. Julien could keep teaching her.

She could keep seeing her tiny brother's uncle. Become part of his life and maybe he would kiss her again…

Alice found she was touching her lips with her fingers as she stood there looking down at the sleeping baby. It took very little imagination to pretend that this feather-light touch was how it had felt when Julien's lips had touched her own.

Suddenly the time that needed to be filled became interminable. There was nothing Alice needed to do unless Jacquot woke again and, with the baby cam handset, she was free to wander anywhere in the house.

Downstairs…where Julien was…

She fought the desire for a while but it got the better of her and eventually Alice crept downstairs with the intention of maybe peeping through the kitchen door. As she got closer, the alluring aroma of roasting meat made her stomach growl so loudly she had to stop and press her hand against her belly, willing it to be silent.

Another few steps and she could hear Julien's voice. He was speaking in French and the tone was confident. Light. As if he was smiling as he spoke?

She had to see. The kitchen door wasn't completely shut and the space inside was brightly lit. Surely nobody would notice if she pushed it open a fraction more and watched for a few minutes?

No heads turned as she pushed the door open further and then Alice forgot to worry about interrupting what was going on. She barely recognised the space. It wasn't so much the professional lights and microphones on the end of long poles that looked as much out of place as the man with a huge camera balanced on his shoulder. It was more that the kitchen had been turned into a Christmas wonderland.

Long ropes of greenery threaded with fairy-lights hung in loops on the walls a little below ceiling height. A tall tree stood in the corner, with tiny lights sparkling amongst red and silver themed decorations, and a wreath of mistletoe hung from a central light fitting. The huge kitchen table had been pushed to one side of the room and decorated as if a family was about to sit down for Christmas dinner.

Fine white china, gleaming silverware and crystal glasses marked each place setting. Christmas crackers with red and silver paper lay beside each plate. There were places for platters of food to rest on wrought-iron trivets and any remaining space on the table was covered with candles in glass holders with wreaths of greenery studded with red berries. The flickering flames of the candles glinted on the silver cutlery and champagne flutes.

There was Christmas music playing softly in the background. Carols that were instantly familiar and beloved to Alice because they were being sung in English. Memories of Christmas dinners shared with her mother and grandmother brought a lump to her throat and Alice had to look away from the table.

To where Julien was standing behind the island bench, smiling into a camera as he spoke. His hair was neatly tied back in the usual ponytail but his face looked different. Had makeup emphasised those thick, dark eyebrows and lashes, the shadowing of his jaw and the beautiful olive tone of his skin or was it the white chef's tunic he was wearing, underneath a striped apron, with the neck unbuttoned and the sleeves rolled up? Maybe the difference was simply that he was smiling in a way Alice hadn't seen. A non-crooked way.

He looked happy. More than that—this was a

man who was sharing something he was totally passionate about. The superb knife skills as he diced an onion and celery sticks and the way he could toss a frying pan full of tiny pieces without spilling a thing might be showmanship but they were as natural as breathing to Julien.

Such a contrast to how she'd seen him standing—bewildered—staring down at his howling nephew when he'd had no idea of what to do.

The sight of him now made her catch her breath but the memory of him holding Jacquot had caught her heart completely.

She might think she'd stayed in control but, in retrospect, that had probably been the moment she'd gone past the point of no return when it came to falling in love with Julien Dubois.

Or had that moment been when she'd caught his gaze when they'd both been under the spell of Jacquot's first smile?

Or maybe when he'd brushed that kiss on her lips this morning?

Trying to identify when it had happened was pointless. It was probably the combination that had filled that jar past bursting point. Alice could almost feel the pieces shattering and the emotions the jar had contained rushing out to fill every cell of her body.

It was creating a heat like nothing she had ever experienced.

Desire that was so much more than purely physical.

She'd never wanted the touch of any man the way she wanted Julien Dubois.

As if he felt the force of that desire, Julien suddenly glanced up from what he was doing and his words stopped in mid-sentence. His hands froze in mid-air just as he was about to add another handful of ingredients to the frying pan and for an insanely long moment it felt as if the world had stopped turning.

He knew exactly what she was thinking and… for that moment Alice could swear he had caught that desire like a match to a fuse and it was about to explode.

The moment was shattered by a bark of incredulous sound that came from a man holding a clipboard and the cameraman sounded like he'd uttered a succinct oath as he lowered his camera to turn and stare at Alice. Filming had clearly been interrupted and it was only then that Alice realised she wasn't peering around the edge of the door any more. When had she stepped right into the kitchen without noticing herself moving? In that delicious stretch of time when her bones had been melting and she'd been unable to think of anything but her longing to be with Julien?

What on earth had she done? Was it possible to pick up filming at the place they had stopped or would they have to film that whole demonstration of preparing whatever it was in the frying pan again? A peek in Julien's direction revealed that he was as angry as everybody else in this space. A girl holding the microphone and somebody else beneath a light stand had moved so they could join in the incredulous staring.

She didn't need to understand a word of French to know that more than one person was telling her to go away and not come back but it was

Julien who made sure she understood by translating.

'Go away, Alice. Do not come near here again.'

It sounded more like *Do not come near me again*.

Mortified, Alice could feel the worst blush ever flood up from her neck into her face. Even her ears felt like they were burning.

'I'm sorry,' she said. 'I'm terribly sorry…'

She closed the kitchen door behind her as she fled.

CHAPTER EIGHT

HEADLONG FLIGHT DIDN'T leave any room for rational thought.

Instead of running upstairs to the safety of the nursery suite, Alice found she had gone in the direction of the first place she'd felt safe in this house.

The conservatory.

The room was dark but there were muted floodlights in the garden that illuminated the swimming pool and filtered in through glass walls to provide a hint of green on the dark shapes of the indoor trees and made the white furniture easy to find. It was the same couch she'd sat on when she had held Jacquot for the first time that Alice chose to curl up on to wait out the shame of the trouble she'd caused.

And the pain of the way Julien had dismissed her.

She'd been remembering her family the last

time she'd come in here alone. The way her mother and grandmother had always been able to know if she wasn't telling the truth. Would they be able to see what felt stupidly like a broken heart right now?

He's French, her grandmother might have sniffed. *What did you expect?*

But her mother? Might she have given her comfort because she would understand? Had André sent her away looking like he'd never wanted to see her again when she had already gifted her heart to him? When she had been carrying his baby in her belly?

She had no idea how long she sat there, failing to win a battle with tears of self-pity, but Alice finally pulled herself together.

It was ridiculous to feel like she had a broken heart. This wasn't a fairy-tale, this house was not a palace and Julien wasn't any kind of fantasy prince. He'd been forced to live in the same house as her with the rest of the world shut away and, yes, there had been moments where she could convince herself that something amazing was happening between them but he was back in his real life now and she had absolutely no part in it. It had been the promise of being able to do that that had led to him kissing her in the first place.

The worst part of it all was that he'd seen the desire that must have been glowing from her face like a neon sign. He'd been so shocked he hadn't been able to look away. It wasn't that he felt the same way at all. He'd been...appalled.

There was no point wallowing in it. It might be as soon as tomorrow that the results of those blood tests came through and that Jacquot would be deemed to be no danger to others. This quarantine would end. Jacquot would be taken into the care of his grandmother and she herself would have to go home and she would never set foot in this house again. The opportunity to find out anything about her father that she couldn't find printed in a magazine or revealed in a television interview would be lost for ever.

Her heart thumping, Alice got to her feet and went to the room that Julien had taken her to when she had first arrived. Flickering screens from the security system showed her where she could turn on a desk lamp rather than the main lights of the room. Even in the soft light the shards of glass still clinging to the oversized portrait of her father was a shocking reminder of that violent action of Julien's and the pent-up grief and hatred it had revealed, but Alice pushed any thoughts of him away. She was here in the hope of finding something that might let her believe her father hadn't been a man worthy of that kind of hatred. Maybe something she could keep to give Jacquot in years to come.

There were stacks of magazines with pictures of André Laurent on their covers. Silver trophies and framed photographs of André with people that Alice could recognise as being famous. Film stars and someone she thought had been a French president. Moving behind the desk, she found a smaller photograph in a heart-shaped silver frame. A much older-looking André with his arms around the waist of a very beautiful, young, dark-haired woman who had to be Julien's sister.

Alice picked up the image and studied it. They

were looking at each other rather than the camera and it was impossible not to catch the impression that they were very much in love. It was a picture of a private moment and it made Alice catch her breath, wishing that the photo of *her* parents had been this revealing.

It was a double frame that could be closed and in the other side was a photo of a baby with tufts of dark hair. Jacquot. Had it been taken on the day he'd been born? When André had lost the mother of the only child he'd known he had? It didn't matter. What did matter was that it showed how important his brand-new family had been to André and it was something that Jacquot would treasure when he was old enough to understand. Alice set the frame carefully to one side of the desk.

She would come and get it when she was leaving the house and then somehow, some time she would find a way to give it to her little brother.

She sat there for a long moment and then idly began opening desk drawers. Maybe she was hoping she might find cards that had been kept with messages of love in them but there seemed to be only stationery items like embossed paper and pens. A lower drawer had a business diary and appointment cards. Plane tickets to Geneva had been booked for Christmas Eve and there were passports with the tickets...two of them. One had a shiny, unmarked cover and had been issued only last week—a baby's first official document.

Alice closed the drawer slowly. Had André been planning a family Christmas to help him get through the grief of this first celebration without his wife? Would Madame Laurent be struggling with her own sadness and that was why she was so eager to collect Jacquot? It could be that she might welcome her as well.

Movement from the screens caught her eye and she watched as the headlights of cars and vans lit up the driveway and went out the gates. The road outside looked empty. Had the media finally given up on getting a story or pictures? It was another clue that normal life would be resumed in the near future but it felt curiously as if something important was slipping through her fingers.

The baby cam monitor showed Jacquot to be sleeping peacefully and maybe it was time for Alice to follow his example. The delicious smell of the Christmas feast that had been prepared in the kitchens should have been just as enticing when Alice reached the foyer but, despite her earlier hunger, her appetite was nothing like it had been when she had come downstairs earlier.

And when she saw who was emerging from the interior kitchen door, it vanished completely.

Julien had shed the striped apron. He'd unbuttoned the white tunic completely so that it hung open and most of his chest was bare. He was wearing faded denim jeans that had been hidden by the apron and maybe he'd kicked his shoes off because his feet were also bare.

And he'd taken the fastening off his ponytail. This was the first time Alice had seen him with his hair loose and she'd been right about how it framed and softened his face and brushed his shoulders in soft waves. It took away that professionally polished look and gave him an almost disreputable edge. A muted but irresistible hint of 'bad boy'.

And then she noticed how tired he looked.

And how his face changed when he saw her.

Her mouth went very dry. 'I'm so sorry, Julien,' she said quietly. 'I hope I didn't disrupt the filming too much.'

He flicked his hand. 'It was of no matter. We redid that part when I could concentrate again. It is finished now and only needs editing.' He was giving her an intense look that Alice couldn't interpret.

'I have never lost my focus like that,' he said, walking slowly towards her. 'What is it about you that can do that to me, Alice McMillan?'

'I…I…' *Have absolutely no idea*, she wanted to say. *Maybe it's the same thing that you do to me…*

Her words had evaporated and she didn't need them anyway because Julien hadn't stopped moving and now he was standing right in front of her. As close as he'd been standing that first night when he'd taken the sample from the inside of her cheek.

Once again, she was aware that she had an impossibly gorgeous man standing close enough to kiss her but this time it wasn't embarrassing. This time it was the most amazing moment of her life because she knew that that was exactly what *was* going to happen.

And it wasn't going to be an afterthought to a friendly kiss on both cheeks. Oh, no… The way Julien's hand slid behind her neck and cradled the back of her head meant that this was going to be a *real* kiss…

Except it wasn't. It was so far away from anything Alice had ever experienced that it was a fairy-tale kiss from a handsome prince. A prince who sensed that her bones were melting and scooped her into his arms and held her against his bare chest as he carried her upstairs and into a room well away from the nursery. It must have been the one he'd chosen on the first night here because it had the black clothes he'd been wearing carelessly thrown over the back of a chair.

The huge four-poster bed fitted right into this fantasy and, if Alice had had any qualms about whether she should let this go any further with a man she'd only met days ago, they vanished the moment Julien laid her on that bed and his lips covered hers again. Had he sensed a heartbeat of indecision? The gentle touch of lips suggested exactly that and the moment Alice knew she was completely lost to this overwhelming desire was the moment that gentleness got edged out by an increasingly fierce passion.

The buttons on her shirt popped open and then his lips were on the swell of her breasts and Julien was telling her how beautiful she was. How irresistible. That he was saying it in French didn't matter. In fact, there could be no other language that could make words like this so compelling. So believable...

How on earth had he been able to focus enough to finish filming that show when all he'd wanted to do had been this from the moment he'd seen her standing in the doorway, looking at him the way she had?

And he wasn't disappointed. *Au contraire*, he might have had a great deal of experience in love-making but it had never been this good. Because he'd never touched or been touched by a Scottish pixie with magic in her eyes. And in her hands. And in the soft sounds she made as she responded to every move he made. The cry she couldn't stifle when he took them both over the edge and into paradise…

She stayed in his arms as he waited for his heart rate and breathing to get back to within normal parameters, her head snuggled in the dip between his shoulder and his heart as if the space had been created for just that purpose.

The silence could have been awkward—as these moments usually were—but it was far from that. It was good. Too good because he felt like he'd like to stay like this for ever, and that meant the moment had to be broken before he had time to think about it any longer.

'*C'etait bien*?' he asked softly. 'It was good?'

'Oh…*oui*…' He could feel the curve of her lips against his chest. *'Je l'aime.'*

It felt like the chuckle came from a place he'd forgotten existed. Amusement that was a mix of pride and a deep fondness and possibly a twinge of sadness as well. The only person in his life who had ever made him feel something like that had been Colette—when she'd been young and trying to do something grown up but could only manage cute. Another silence fell, which made him wonder if Alice was trying to think of something else she could say in his language. Instead, the silence was broken by the loud growl of her stomach, which made him smile again.

'You are hungry, *chérie*. I happen to know where there is a Christmas dinner that will still be warm. *Est-ce que tu voudrais diner avec moi?*'

Some of the food had been left in one of the massive ovens to stay warm.

Apparently more than one version of things had been cooked because the filming had needed different stages of the cooking process within a short time period. Most of it was stored in the cold room now and Julien warned Alice that she might be eating Christmas dinner more than once.

Alice sat at the end of the table with a flute of champagne in her hand and watched as Julien placed platter after platter of amazing-looking food in the spaces between the dozens of flickering candles.

A turkey and a jug of aromatic gravy with a curl of steam above it. Wedges of roasted pumpkin and crispy, browned potatoes. Sweet glazed carrots and Brussels sprouts. Bread sauce.

'Oh…you did pigs in blankets. My absolute favourite.' Alice picked up one of the tiny sausages wrapped in bacon and baked until crisp. 'Oh, yum. How do you say "yum" in French?'

Julien had a carving knife in one hand and a sharpening steel in the other. '*Miam-miam,*' he told her.

He'd just put his faded jeans and his black shirt on before they'd left his bedroom and the shirt was only buttoned halfway up but it didn't matter that he wasn't wearing his white tunic or even that he hadn't tied back his hair again once he began sharpening that knife. He was every inch the professional chef and this had to be the sexiest thing Alice had ever seen a man doing.

Her pig in its blanket remained barely tasted and her champagne was forgotten. The pleasure Alice was getting from simply watching Julien was as much as she could cope with because it took far more than just her eyes. Her whole body was watching and remembering every touch he had given her. Every stroke and every kiss and— if she never experienced it again—she would never forget this blissful afterglow if she lived to be a hundred and two.

With the succulent meat carved and served, Julien piled their plates with a sample of everything else he had cooked for his traditional British Christmas dinner.

Alice wondered what the other chef had done for his French version but she didn't want the conversation to turn professional. She wanted to bask in this delicious glow for a little longer. To talk about things that mattered only to themselves.

But she didn't want to say too much either. Whatever was happening here was new and fragile and there was a danger of breaking it with the pressure of words that were too heavy or smothering it with a layer of too much emotion. Maybe talking about food was safer.

'This is the best Christmas dinner I've ever tasted,' she told him. 'As much as I adored my mum and my gran, they could never cook like this. The turkey was always dry.'

'Putting butter under the skin makes a difference. This is how I do it in my restaurant.'

'Are you open on Christmas Day?'

'No. But we serve Christmas meals for two or even three weeks of December. By the time Christmas Day comes, the last thing I want to eat is a goose. Or a turkey.'

'So what do you cook to celebrate Christmas Day?'

Julien shrugged. 'It's not something I celebrate.

It means nothing to me other than a day to be alone and rest.'

Alice stopped eating. So there was no significant other in his life who he would spend a special day with? It should be a relief to know that but, instead, it was almost frightening. Was Julien a lone wolf? Was he alone by a choice that was unlikely to change? She stared at her half-eaten meal but, however delicious it was, she had no inclination to eat anything more.

'What about when you were a child?'

Julien followed her example and put down his fork, picking up his glass instead. 'Celebrations were something to be feared when I was a child.'

There was nothing Alice could find to say in response. She could only look at Julien's face in the soft light of the candles and hold her breath until the ache in her chest eased a little.

Julien drained his glass of champagne and reached for one of the bottles of wine on the table. The ruby-red liquid filled the crystal glass and he offered it to Alice but she shook her head, remaining silent as he closed his eyes and took a long sip of his wine. And then another. And then he opened his eyes again but kept his gaze on the glass in his hand as he began talking quietly.

'My father walked out on us when I was five years old. He'd married my mother because she was pregnant but he told us many times that he'd never wanted a child. When it became apparent that another child was on the way, it was too much and he left.'

'Oh, *Julien*...'

Alice's heart ached for that little boy who'd known he hadn't been wanted. Who had probably believed that it was his fault that his father had abandoned them.

'My mother couldn't cope alone so she married again as soon as she could. She chose an angry man who could use words as well as his fists as weapons and the worst times were always when he drank too much. Celebrations like birthdays and especially Christmas were the days he always drank too much.'

As if the reminder disgusted him, Julien put his glass down and pushed it away. 'It's too easy to hurt a child,' he murmured. 'That's why I will never have one of my own.'

The ache around Alice's heart took on a hollow edge as if it was surrounded by a bottomless pit. 'But you have Jacquot now. You are his guardian...'

'Which means I have to ensure that he is safe and cared for. I can't bring up a child. I work long hours in my restaurant. I have to travel a lot for my television work and my recipe books. Other time is taken up with production and editing. It would be impossible to live with a baby.'

'But he has to be *loved*,' Alice whispered. 'That's just as important as being safe and cared for. Maybe *more* important.' She'd seen how much it had meant to him that Colette's precious rabbit toy had been bequeathed to her baby. And the way Julien had looked when Jacquot had smiled at them both. 'You said he looks like Colette and...and I know you loved your sister...'

He must have loved her very much to have dropped out of school to protect her from their stepfather.

'How old were you when your mother died?' Alice asked, when Julien said nothing.

'Fifteen.'

'And Colette was…?'

'Ten. A child.'

He hadn't been much more than a child himself. 'And you were allowed to be Colette's guardian when you were so young?'

'I would have lied about my age if anyone had asked but it turned out there was nobody who cared enough to find out.'

'That must have been *so* hard…'

Julien picked up one of the pigs in blankets from his plate with his fingers and bit into it, tilting his head to shrug off her comment.

'I worked,' he said a moment later. 'First one job and then two. Even three at one time. I had found a cheap apartment for us. Colette went to school and she looked after herself after school. She knew it was the only way we could stay together. We were the only family we each had. We had to help one another.' He looked at the food in his hand and then put it down, as though his appetite had vanished.

'It only worked because she was old enough to do that,' he added. 'I couldn't have cared for a baby then. I couldn't now.'

'You *could*...' Alice whispered. 'If you wanted to.' *If I helped you...*

But her offer remained unspoken because Julien had raised his hand as if warning her off.

'I *don't* want to. I've been down that path before. Tried to protect someone and keep them safe and...and I did not do it well enough... *C'est tout.*'

Alice could hear the pain in his words. He had loved his sister so much. She didn't understand why he was taking so much blame for her death but maybe it was because it was still so recent. Grief was not helpful to rational thinking, was it?

She spoke quietly into the silence.

'She knew how amazing it was—what you did for her. That's why she made you the guardian of her child.'

Julien gave that half-shrug. This wasn't something he really wanted to analyse. 'So she said. I think I told you that she came to see me just before her baby was due to be born. She wanted to give me the legal document about the guardianship. It was the first time I'd seen her in more than a year. Since she'd married André. A marriage that I'd tried to stop.'

'Why?'

'Because he was far too old for her. And he was well known for his excesses. Fast cars. Beautiful women. Too much alcohol...'

So this was why he blamed himself? Because he hadn't protected her from a relationship that had led to a baby's birth that had proved fatal? It wasn't logical. It wasn't even acceptable. 'But they loved each other.'

'Pfff...' The sound was as dismissive as when Julien had made it in response to her suggesting that her mother had been in love with André.

Julien had been both a brother and a parent to his sister and he knew about that kind of protective love, but had anyone ever protected *him*? Did he even realise it could be safe, given that his parents had failed him and even his beloved sister had walked away from his life when he'd thought he was still protecting her? Had he ever allowed himself to be *in* love? Or *felt* truly loved by someone?

It would seem not.

What on earth made her think she had any chance of breaking through a barrier like that?

It would need a miracle.

But miracles did happen sometimes, didn't they? And what better time of year to find one than at Christmas?

There was a clock ticking, though, and it wasn't just counting down the hours until Christmas Day.

And miracles needed to be planted to have any hope of growing.

Alice took a deep breath.

'If you're Jacquot's guardian, you will get to choose who can raise him, won't you?'

'That's my hope. And if it's away from the Laurent family I will still be able to visit him. To watch over him as he grows up and help when or if I'm needed.'

'He needs to be with someone who loves him,' Alice said again. 'I love him. He's my brother. Choose me, Julien.'

He met her gaze and Alice's heart skipped a beat.

But then, after a long moment, he looked away. '*Non. C'est impossible.*'

CHAPTER NINE

THOSE EYES…

He would never forget how they looked in this moment. He had crushed something beautiful. Naïve perhaps but something so genuine that it felt like he was hurting a child by not protecting it from the harshness of reality.

'*Je suis vraiment désolé, chérie*…I am truly sorry…'

He touched her face as he spoke and the way she tilted her head to press her cheek against his fingers was heart-breaking.

He had to take his hand away before he gave in to the urge to hold her in his arms and start kissing her. Promising her things that it would be foolish to even consider. He used his hand to massage his own temples as he let his breath out in a sigh.

'You are single, yes? You don't have a boy-friend or fiancé?'

The blush was a display of intense emotion he was getting used to from Alice. That flash of pain that could also be anger made him realise how stupid the question was. She had just given him more in bed than any woman ever had. And this was Alice. She did not have a deceitful bone in her body. She would never cheat on any man.

'You work as a teacher. You love your work?'

'Yes, but—'

'But you would sacrifice your lifestyle in order to care for a child?'

'Isn't that what you did for your sister?'

Julien shook off what sounded like admiration. He had only done what he'd had to do. And he hadn't done it well enough, anyway.

'You would not be viewed as a suitable guard-ian to raise a baby,' he said. 'And you would want to take him out of the country.'

'Not necessarily.'

'You have a house in Scotland, yes?'

'Yes...'

'Jacquot is French. The last member of what has been a very powerful family in France. His father has always been adored as a national icon.'

'But didn't you say that Madame Laurent lives in Geneva?'

'The border between France and Geneva is merely a formality for many French people. Besides, it is only one of her houses. I understand she has a luxury apartment in Cannes and she may choose to live here in *this* house, which I believe was the family home when André was a child himself.'

A house they both knew was a mausoleum totally unsuited to raising a child.

'I could live in France.' There was determination in those liquid brown eyes now. Passion even. 'I'm half-French.'

'That would be difficult. You don't speak our language.'

Her chin lifted. 'I'm learning.'

She was. The shy echo of her words when he'd asked whether their lovemaking had been good—

Je l'aime—gave him an odd tightness in his chest that made it hard to draw in a new breath.

'Yvonne Laurent is a powerful woman who is used to getting her own way. I don't even know if I can win what I want to get from her. It may be up to the courts to decide whether the relationship of an uncle is more important than that of a grandmother.'

'I'm his sister...'

'A half-sister. And that would probably have to be endorsed by a court as well. The French legal system can be very slow. Especially if someone has the money to delay proceedings. Cases can drag on for months. Years even, and that would not be a good thing for a child. Small children can understand more than you might think...'

Like he had when he'd started protecting Colette from the moment she'd been born? So she would never know that it was also her fault that their father had gone?

He could see the empathy in her eyes now. He shouldn't have told her so much about his childhood. She could read between lines, couldn't she?

She knew how bad it had been and she wanted to make it better somehow.

To make him feel loved?

The pull was so powerful it was painful but he couldn't give in to it. There was no room in his life for someone to be that close. No room in a heart that was too scarred to love and lose again.

'But you are going to fight,' Alice said softly. 'To get what you want. Custody of Jacquot?'

'No.' Julien shook his head. That would mean he would become a parent again. He would have the kind of responsibility he had already proved with his sister that he could not honour well enough. 'I simply want regular access. For the boy to know I am his mother's brother and that I will help him in whatever way he needs as he grows up.'

'Maybe I could have access, too?'

He had to admire her optimism. The hope she could find in every dark corner. Like the way she had seen something good in an ancient toy that was waiting patiently to be of importance one day.

'Maybe fighting isn't the way to win,' Alice said slowly. 'This woman doesn't know that she is my grandmother. If Jacquot is so important to her, it could be that she might listen to her other grandchild. If I don't threaten her, maybe I can persuade her.'

'*Peut-être.*' Alice McMillan could probably persuade anybody if she looked at them like that. He was in danger of being persuaded that he could gift his heart to someone again and he knew that wasn't true. He had found the safe place to be years ago. Away from someone who would see him as a husband and father.

He needed to break the spell that was being woven around him here, in the light of all these romantic candles. In a kitchen that was a room that would always feel like home, no matter where he was. In a Christmas setting that was always redolent with the idea of family...

'Have you had enough to eat? There is a plum pudding with brandy sauce. And custard. Would you like to taste it?'

'*Peut-être,*' Alice enunciated again, carefully.

And then she smiled at him. 'Actually, yes, please. I would love to.'

It was good to move. To take the plates of their unfinished first course away and make a clear space to start again. To move on.

A little showmanship with the pudding came as naturally as breathing these days and it was comforting, too, because it was a demonstration of who he was. What his life was about.

He put the pudding on its platter in front of Alice and moved a candle closer. He held a silver ladle full of brandy over the flame of the candle to warm it and then tipped it just enough to catch the flame and ignite. He never got tired of the magic of that blue flame and the way it flowed so dramatically over the curve of the pudding as he slowly poured it.

'*Oh...*' Alice's gasp of appreciation was another echo of their time in his bed and Julien couldn't dampen a hunger that had nothing to do with food.

He stayed quiet as he served their dessert but Alice had something to say.

'It won't be long, will it? Until…until our quarantine is over.'

'No. I'm hoping the test results will come through tomorrow. I hope also that they are good because I have to go to Paris the next day. It's Christmas Eve and I need to be present on the live broadcast of the show if possible. To appear by a remote connection would not be good enough.'

'Hmm…' Alice paused, a spoonful of pudding halfway to her lips. 'We only have a short time together, then…'

'This is true.' He couldn't tell her that her words gave him a sinking feeling, as if a huge stone had lodged in his gut. To imagine there could be any time together after this was as impossible as the notion of her becoming the guardian for her little brother.

Alice's head was bent, her gaze on her spoon. And then she peeped up through a thick tangle of dark lashes with a look that would have rendered any red-blooded male completely helpless. 'We should make the most of it, then…'

Julien took the spoon gently from her fingers. He cupped her chin and raised it so that he could kiss her with equal gentleness.

'Je suis d'accord. Absolument.'

It couldn't do any real harm, could it? To enjoy the company of such an intriguing woman? At least, this time, he wouldn't have to make the decision to walk away—the way he always did when a woman was getting too close. It was going to happen naturally so why not make the most of every moment they had left? It might only be a matter of hours.

Starting with what was left of this already remarkable night. With luck, Jacquot was well enough to sleep in his own bed right through until morning as long as he was fed and clean and, thanks to the baby monitor, there was no need for Alice to return to *her* own bed.

He was more than happy to share his.

It was the first time little Jacquot Laurent had slept through the night.

It was also the first time he had woken and

not immediately cried for attention. Instead, the sounds that came through the monitor handset were soft chirrups and coos, as if the baby was experimenting with talking to himself.

Alice awoke to the sounds with a smile already curving her lips. And then she realised she was still snuggled against Julien's bare chest with his arm around her and his fingers carelessly draped across her breast and the smile seemed to turn inwards.

She had never felt contentment like this. A weariness that felt blissful because of what had been experienced instead of sleep. Alice tilted her head so that she could see Julien's face. Relaxed in slumber, he had lost the solemn air and intensity she had grown accustomed to. A tress of that surprisingly soft hair had caught on his lashes and lay across his cheek and lips. Alice reached up and gently brushed it back into place. Maybe her grandmother would have disapproved of Julien's hairstyle but Alice was never going to forget the thrilling tickle of that hair on her skin when Julien had been kissing and tasting her body. Her neck…her breasts…her belly… and, *oh*…

A pair of gorgeous hazel eyes were on her face and Alice knew she was going to blush so she ducked her head.

'Jacquot is awake. Listen…'

Julien also smiled. 'He sounds happy.'

'He must be hungry. I need to go to him.'

'Of course. And I should go and do something with that disaster of a kitchen. Shall I bring you some coffee before breakfast?'

'Please…' Alice rolled away but Julien's arm tightened around her and pulled her back.

'You have forgotten something, *chérie*.'

'Oh? What?'

'This…' Julien kissed her. A brief caress and then a more thorough one. 'It is a French custom, the morning kiss…'

'Mmm…' If it hadn't been for a more demanding cry coming from the monitor, the morning kiss would no doubt have become much more than that.

Was it too much to hope that they could have

one more night together? Alice wondered as she hastily pulled on her clothes and made her way to the nursery. This felt like the start of something new. Something wonderful. Something that was too good to be true?

She heard the phone ringing as she had Jacquot in his bath, squeaking the rubber duck to make him smile and kick his feet. Was it nine a.m. already? The doctor was as reliable as an alarm clock. She had her little brother dressed and ready for his new day by the time Julien came to the nursery, carrying a steaming mug of delicious-smelling coffee. A wide grin appeared on the baby's face.

'He knows you,' Alice said. 'Here…he needs a cuddle from his uncle.' She took the mug of coffee from his hand and eased the bundle of baby into Julien's arms. Neither of them made any protest about the contact and Alice beamed at them both before taking her first sip of coffee.

This was progress. If Julien could bond with Jacquot as much as she had, they could join forces to make sure this baby had what he needed so badly—people to love him to bits.

'Was it the doctor who rang? Did you tell him how happy Jacquot sounded this morning?'

'It was and I did. He said that there doesn't need to be any further restriction to keeping him in the house if he's well enough to go out.'

'Oh…' That meant that he could be taken out, didn't it? Taken away…

'He also said that the results of our blood tests are finally back. We are both immune to measles. There are no further restrictions on either of us either. I have already booked an early flight to Paris tomorrow morning. And…'

Alice held her breath. Julien was looking down at the baby in his arms, who must have been enjoying the sound of his voice as much as she was because he smiled again, so energetically it made his whole little body wiggle. And Julien was smiling back but then he looked up at Alice and his smile faded.

'And Madame Laurent is driving down from Geneva this afternoon to make arrangements.

She intends to take Jacquot back to her home tonight.'

The lump in Alice's throat was too big to swallow. 'What time is she due to arrive?'

'I'm not sure. Early this evening, I expect.' Julien's face was as sombre as the first time she'd met him but there was a depth of softness there that was very new. 'I'm sorry, *chérie*...there seems to be nothing I can do to stop this. Nothing I can do to help you.'

Alice looked away as she blinked back tears but all she could think about was the man standing there, holding the small baby. They were both the people she now cared about more than anyone else in her world.

And she had less than a day to be with them both. She pulled in a shaky breath.

'There is one thing you could do.'

'What is that? I have a few urgent matters I must attend to first, like discussing how to handle this with my solicitor, but I will have time this afternoon. If I can do this thing for you, I promise you I will.'

Alice turned back. 'I will have to leave France tomorrow and I feel like I haven't seen nearly enough. Could you take me somewhere that I will remember? Maybe somewhere...' her voice became quieter, hopeful '...that is special to you?'

She saw a flicker of doubt in his eyes. Was he reluctant to let her any further into his life?

'We would have to take the little one with us.'

Alice nodded. 'I know where things are. Like the nappy bag and a pram. Or there's a front pack. I can make up a bottle of formula that any café could warm for us.' She bit her lip. 'Have those journalists gone? You don't get harassed in public for being famous, do you?'

'I know how to deal with that.' His expression changed. A decision had been made and there was a hint of a smile on his lips. 'And I think I know where I can take you. Somewhere special enough for your last day in France. I will attend to what I must do and you get yourself and Jacquot ready.'

Alice took the baby from his arms and smiled up at him. 'Will I like it?'

'You will love it.' He turned to leave the nursery.

'You have forgotten something, Julien.'

'Oh…?'

Alice stood on tiptoe, leaning over the baby to kiss him. 'It's a Scottish custom,' she said softly. 'The goodbye kiss…'

It was even better than the kiss, she decided moments later—the way she'd made him smile.

Some time out to clear his head was the best thing he could do for this afternoon. After a string of telephone conversations between himself, his solicitor and Madame Laurent's solicitor, it had been agreed that a brief family meeting might be the best first step. Nothing official, such as taking Jacquot away from the house, would happen before tomorrow.

This was the opportunity Julien had requested for the key players to discuss the situation without outside input and legal arguments to inflame

tempers. Alice's words had stayed in his mind—
that perhaps persuasion might be more effective
than threats. He had called for a temporary truce
and, amazingly, Madame Laurent had agreed.
The only thing she didn't know was that there
were now three key players rather than two. And
that the third one was a granddaughter she didn't
know existed.

Alice could either be an ace up his sleeve or be
seen as a threat that could close doors for ever.
It was impossible to know which way the dice
might roll but Julien was trying to channel some
of Alice's optimism. It might help all of them.

Being recognised was not usually a problem
and the media contingent outside the gates had
given up and gone elsewhere days ago but Julien did need to be careful this time. He was
breaching the court order that the Laurent family solicitors had arrived with on the day of the
funeral to prevent him taking his nephew anywhere, and there was still the problem of Alice's
connection to the family becoming public before
Yvonne Laurent had time to accept the bomb-

shell. It might have been easier to stay discreetly in the house for one more day but he'd made a promise and he was not about to dishonour that.

So he wore a black fisherman-style pullover under a coat with its collar turned up and hid his hair beneath a black woollen beanie that he wore low on his forehead because the day was too overcast to warrant sunglasses. Fortunately the chances of being recognised were low anyway, because the last thing anybody would expect would be to see him out with a woman who had a baby in a front pack, well bundled up for any winter chill with tiny arms and legs poking out of the contraption like a miniature snowman.

It hadn't been hard to think of an appropriate place to take Alice to give her a taste of France at Christmastime. He and Colette had been taken there once, as children, and it was probably the happiest memory of his entire childhood.

It was a bonus that the clouds were thick and dark enough to make it seem much later in the day than early afternoon because it made the Christmas lights of Nice's *marché de Noël* almost as bright as they would be at night. The enormous pine trees along the Promenade du Paillon were thickly dusted with artificial snow as they walked through the park to the Place Massena, and as they got closer they could see that the ice-skating rink was full of families out with their children and the giant Ferris wheel was turning. The massive Christmas trees were sparkling and there were crowds of shoppers at the stalls selling hand-crafted gifts and food and mulled wine.

And Alice looked as excited by it all as Colette had been when she'd still been a small child of about seven or eight. Those brown eyes that had captured him from the moment he'd seen them produce tears in André's office that first day were shining with joy now and Julien felt his chest expand with his own pleasure in having chosen this experience as his gift for her last day here.

That she was here with her baby brother in her arms made it even more special.

'Stand here, so that the Ferris wheel and the Christmas trees are behind you. I will take a photo for you.'

He would keep a copy of that photograph himself. If the sadness from the past tried to suck him back, he would be able to look at that smile and remember his Scottish pixie, who could always find something to celebrate.

He was missing Alice already. How stupid was that?

Would she miss him? Would she remember this time with him? Maybe a memento would help. A gift from one of the stalls perhaps?

Alice had turned to watch the Ferris wheel. Or was she watching the people on the skating rink? It was a colourful scene. There were coloured lights around the edges of the rink and overhead. Many people were dressed in Christmas shades of bright red and green and most of them were wearing Santa hats or reindeer horns. The people closest to them right now were a man and a woman who were holding the mittened hands of a small boy as he wobbled on his skates between them. A family, enjoying a Christmas outing. If she could have what she was wishing for, Julien thought, that could be Alice in a few years' time, with the father figure she chose to share her life with as she raised her baby brother.

The thought sat uneasily. He didn't want to imagine Alice with another man but it was inevitable, wasn't it? What man could resist those eyes? That spirit of optimism or that generosity as a lover? And it was no more than she deserved—to find that man and have babies of her own to cherish. He had no right to feel the way he did. Resentful almost?

Julien shook off the unwelcome train of his thoughts. He was here to give Alice a happy memory of France. He went to take her hand so that he could lead her towards the stalls and find a gift but her hands were busy, adjusting the straps of the front pack.

'Is it heavy? Would you like me to take him for a while?'

There was surprise in her eyes. And then something he couldn't identify but it looked curiously like satisfaction.

'Yes, please,' she said. '*Merci beaucoup*, Julien.'

* * *

It felt completely natural to take Julien's hand, once the front pack was securely in place and his hands were free. There was so much to look at as they wove their way slowly through the crowds, admiring the goods on offer at the stalls, but Alice kept looking sideways.

Was there anything more appealing than the sight of a tall, broad-shouldered man with a tiny baby on his chest?

And when you loved them both, was there anything that could make you feel more like your heart was so full it might simply break from joy?

She needed to find something else to look at before that joy escaped as tears.

'Oh, look…those hats have sparkles. Aren't they pretty?'

They were only woollen hats but they had large diamantes glued all over them and soft, furry pompoms on the top.

'Would you like one?' There was a furrow just visible under Julien's hat. 'I hadn't noticed that you didn't have a hat. Are your ears cold?'

'No, but I would love a hat anyway.' As much as she loved the concern in his voice and the idea that he cared if her ears were cold or not. 'The sparkle would always remind me of where it came from and when.'

'What colour would you like?'

'Black.' There was no hesitation on Alice's part. It would match Julien's hat but with a bonus. 'It makes the sparkles stand out more.'

Julien spoke to the woman running the stall and money changed hands. Instead of having the hat put into a bag, he put it on Alice's head, tucking her hair back from her face. Then he touched her nose with his finger.

'*Très mignon*,' he pronounced. 'Very cute. *Tout comme tu.*'

The stall owner said something then and Alice saw the warmth in his eyes vanish.

She nudged Julien. 'What did she say?'

He shook his head, turning away. Confused, Alice glanced back at the woman. Her confusion was being reflected back at her and the woman raised her hands in a puzzled gesture.

ALISON ROBERTS 215

'I say only that he has a beautiful wife and the most beautiful baby in the world.'

Oh… That would have been a shock to a man who was a lone wolf and had decided long ago that he would never have a child of his own. No wonder the pleasure of this outing began to fade. When Jacquot finally woke a short time later and let them know he was hungry and needed changing, it was obvious that Julien was relieved to hand the baby back to Alice.

And the spell was broken. Even the lights and music and the crowd of happy people couldn't fix what had been broken and it was Alice's turn to feel relieved when Julien suggested it was time to go back to the house.

They drove back in Julien's car in silence and he used a remote to open those extraordinarily ornate gates that had been Alice's first glimpse of this property.

It was only the second time she had passed through these gates into her father's estate. The first had been nearly a week ago but it felt like for ever because of how it had changed her life.

It felt like yesterday, too, because that time was etched into her memory for ever. She'd been so hopeful on her arrival but nervous as well. There'd been the media crowd to get through, helicopters hovering overhead and a grim man who'd met her at the door.

How different things were now. The media had given up and gone. There were no helicopters and she'd seen through the grimness that Julien had been wearing like a cloak to cover the vulnerability of a man who was capable of loving greatly but only felt safe to pour that passion into his work.

A man she had utterly fallen in love with.

But she felt far more nervous than she had that first time she'd been escorted up this driveway because there was a car parked on the curve of the driveway where it looped past the front doors to the mansion. A huge, gleaming black car. The kind that a very wealthy woman might be chauffeured to her desired destination in. The chauffeur was still sitting in the car but the back seat was empty.

Madame Laurent had clearly arrived and must have had a key to her son's house. She was waiting for them inside.

The nerves were there because Alice knew that this perfect day was almost over. That—very soon—she might have to say goodbye to both the man and baby she loved so much.

But the woman waiting for them was also the grandmother she had never met.

There was still a glimmer of hope.

CHAPTER TEN

Yvonne Laurent was a perfect example of aristocratic elegance.

A tall, slim woman with beautifully coiffed silver hair and expertly applied make-up, she was wearing a twin set and pearls beneath the jacket and skirt of a tailored suit.

Alice was still wearing her forest-green jumper over one of the two shirts she'd been washing out every day and the jeans that were probably overdue for a wash were tucked into boots that had been getting a little more scuffed every day. And she had a silly hat with a pompom and sparkles on her head.

The visitor awaiting their arrival in the foyer barely gave her—or Jacquot—a second glance.

'*Bonjour*, Julien.' Her voice was as measured and controlled as her appearance but Alice understood nothing more than the greeting as a rapid conversation followed the polite kissing on each cheek. Julien ushered the older woman into the drawing room opposite the entrance to the grand salon and then turned back to Alice.

'She thinks you're a nanny,' he said in a low voice. 'I will explain why you are really here but it may be best if you take the little one up to the nursery in the meantime.'

Her nod of acquiescence was stiff. She could excuse the lack of interest in someone thought to be no more than hired help but she had this woman's grandchild cuddled against her chest and Madame Laurent had made no effort to try and see the baby's face. And this was supposed to be her precious grandchild that she was determined to care for?

The hope that she might welcome an adult granddaughter was evaporating. It was a relief to go upstairs. To change Jacquot and hold him in her arms while she fed him his bottle. To sing to him softly as she tucked him into his cot for what was possibly going to be the last time.

To wait. It felt like her future was lying in the hands of others but there was nothing she could do but wait.

And hope…

'Madame Laurent…I'm sorry that it has taken circumstances like this to meet you.'

She'd been at Colette's funeral, of course, but she'd been by André's side and Julien had kept his distance. He hadn't been welcome. At his own *sister's* funeral…

He couldn't afford to let any bitterness loose right now, however. And they were both dealing with the grief of losing a loved one. Surely that gave them a connection that would allow persuasion rather than threats—as Alice had suggested?

'I realise that this is a difficult time for you,' he said quietly. 'I am truly sorry for your loss, *madame.*'

The pale blue eyes he was looking into filled with tears. Yvonne Laurent lowered herself onto the overstuffed cushion of a small couch and opened her handbag to extract an embroidered handkerchief that she pressed to a corner of one eye and then the other. Finally, she spoke.

'My grandson is the only family I have left in the world.'

'Indeed.' Julien sat on the edge of another couch, facing her. This certainly wasn't the time to tell her that she was wrong. That she actually had another grandchild.

'It is the same for me, *madame*. Which is why I hope we can find agreement to keep him safe. Cared for. Loved…' The last word brought another echo of Alice's voice to the back of his mind. It felt like she was here in the room with him and it made it all the more important to make this work.

Even Madame Laurent's sniff was elegant. This time she pressed the handkerchief to her nose.

'That is exactly what I will do for Jacques. I am the one who can care for an infant. You… you have important work that must keep you extremely busy. You would not have the time for such a young child.'

Julien stiffened. He could *make* time, if he had to.

'You are a national icon, Julien.' Yvonne looked up to meet his gaze and her smile was poignant. 'My son was also. I understand the kind of pressure that goes with such a status.' When she blinked, her eyes glistened with tears again. 'I adored my son. I will give the same love and attention to my beloved grandson. I will provide the best nannies. Find the best schools.'

Julien dipped his head in acknowledgment. He could well believe that no money would be spared in providing for Jacquot but that wasn't the point.

'He's my nephew. My sister's child. I want to be part of his life.'

'Of course…' There was empathy in her tone now. 'I understand how important that is. I know there were…ah…difficulties in your relationship with my son but that is of little consequence now. This is about what is best for Jacques, is it not?'

'Yes.' Julien hadn't expected Madame Laurent to be so accommodating. He found himself smiling at her.

'I am not a young woman,' she said. 'While I can, of course I wish to provide a home for my grandson but I know there will come a time when he needs more than a safe nursery. A time when he needs a father figure. A time…' her indrawn breath was shaky '…when I will not be here to help him.'

'I want him to know who I am. I want to be part of his life.'

Madame Laurent tilted her head. 'You may visit whenever your schedule makes it possible. You will be made welcome at my estate.'

'And if anything happens to make it impossible for you to care for him?'

'I hope that will not be for a long time but, in that event, your guardianship will take priority.' Yvonne Laurent tucked her handkerchief back into her handbag. She got to her feet. 'If you're happy, I will have all of this documented by my solicitors and will bring the papers with me to-morrow when I come to collect my grandson.'

Happy? He should be. Madame Laurent had just agreed to everything he'd been trying to win when he'd come here in the first place. More, even. To be assigned indisputable guardianship of Jacquot if it became necessary in the future was an insurance policy that made this better than he could have hoped. But something was stopping any personal celebration and he knew what that something was.

Alice.

'Before you go, *madame*, there is something I should tell you about.'

'Oh…?'

'You have more than your grandson here in this house.' Julien took a deep breath. 'You also have a granddaughter.'

Madame Laurent stared at him. '*Non…c'est impossible…*'

Alice felt like she'd been waiting for ever.

Had Julien told Madame Laurent that she now had two grandchildren? Should she go downstairs? Brushing her hair, Alice wished she had packed some more clothes other than a spare shirt and clean underwear for this trip. Not that she owned anything like a power suit herself but why hadn't she thought to include a dress? Because she hadn't thought to present anything other than who she really was when she'd come in search of her father and that how the package was wrapped was of no importance?

Julien had seen through her lack of designer wear and sophistication. Or had he? If she had simply been a diversion from the boredom of being confined, it wouldn't have mattered what she looked like. Considering her an acceptable companion in the kind of world he normally inhabited might be a very different matter, especially if the people in that world were anything like Madame Laurent. And if they were, a tiny voice whispered, would she even want to be there?

It needed every ounce of her courage to make the decision to go downstairs. Alice retrieved the photograph of her parents from her backpack, pushing aside the memory of how Julien had initially dismissed this evidence of her mother's relationship with André. The DNA test had been done and there could be no dismissal now. She hesitated a few moments more, however, checking—as she always did—that the baby cam was on and working before leaving the nursery.

But she didn't even get as far as the door because it was blocked by someone coming in.

Madame Laurent.

'Miss McMillan, it appears that you have a very unexpected connection with the Laurent family.'

Her English was so perfect it had virtually no accent and it made Alice realise how much she loved the way Julien spoke her language and could make it sound so much softer and almost as musical and inviting as his native tongue. How much she loved the way he said her name. It made the way this woman spoke seem so much harsher. Controlled and clipped. Cold...

She looked past Madame Laurent's shoulder in the hope that Julien had come upstairs as well but the doorway and the gallery beyond were empty.

She was alone. With her grandmother.

'I...I'm very happy to meet you,' she said quietly. 'I'm so very sorry for your loss. It's been devastating for me to have come here too late to be able to meet my father.'

Yvonne was staring at her but there was no more warmth in either her expression or her body language than there had been in her voice. Then her gaze ran down the length of Alice's body, pausing as it reversed its journey.

'What is that?'

'Oh… It's a photograph. The only one I have of my parents together. It's what made me come here…' It was a wonder Alice's hand wasn't shaking as she held it out. 'Would you like to see?'

The focus of this woman's stare was unnerving.

'Her name was Jeannette McMillan. She came to work here in a gap year when she was eighteen. It was where she met your son, André.' Alice knew she was speaking too fast. Saying too much, but she needed desperately to break through what seemed an impenetrable barrier. 'Where she fell in love…'

Yvonne Laurent's breath was expelled in a dismissive snort. An echo of Julien's reaction. Was it a cultural thing to discount an extreme emotional connection? Surely not. Everybody knew that Paris was the city of love.

'I remember her.' The words dripped ice. The glance Alice received then sent a chill down her spine.

'I fail to understand what went wrong. The arrangements had been made. I had paid their exorbitant fees myself so that the unfortunate pregnancy could be dealt with discreetly.'

The mix of emotion that hit Alice was peculiar. There was anger that someone had been prepared to pay a lot of money to make sure she didn't exist. But there was a flash of something close to joy there as well. So it hadn't been her father who'd been the driving force in trying to get rid of her? It had been *this* woman. Her grandmother.

'*I* was that pregnancy,' she said slowly. 'And I was loved. By my mother. And by my *other* grandmother.'

Any rebuke her words held fell on deaf ears.

The huge diamonds in her rings flashed in the soft light of the nursery as Madame Laurent smoothed her perfectly groomed hair.

'I should sue that clinic,' she said. 'They told me the procedure had been completed. That the girl had been sent out of the country and would no longer be a problem.'

'Maybe they took pity on my mother when they saw how frightened she was. Or how much she wanted the baby of the man she loved.' Alice's voice was low. She was talking aloud to herself rather than trying to make conversation with someone she now knew she could never connect with.

Another derisive sound from Yvonne Laurent made her lift her chin and stare back at her, probably with the same kind of disgusted look she had been subjected to herself. This was unexpectedly devastating and a part of her needed to hit back.

'Perhaps it was André who made different arrangements,' she said. 'Perhaps he paid the clinic an even more exorbitant fee so that he could keep my mother safe. From *you*...'

'No. My son would not have done that. His racing career was everything to him. He was young. He could not have kept doing it if I hadn't provided the funding and he knew that was going to stop if he had anything more to do with a—a *waitress* who'd been stupid enough to try and catch him by producing an unwanted brat. She wasn't the only one. He was pursued by a great many like her. *Les salopes*... Trash...'

Alice stepped back as if she could get out of range of such venom. Her steps took her closer to the cot where Jacquot lay sleeping. It was then that fear stepped in. Not for herself—it didn't matter what this woman thought of her—but she was suddenly and dreadfully afraid for this innocent baby who was in danger of being brought up by a woman who was giving every impression that she was incapable of compassion, let alone love.

'And Jacquot?' she heard herself whisper. 'Is *he* an unwanted "brat" as well?'

'Of course not,' Yvonne Laurent snapped. 'He is a legitimate child and the heir to the Laurent name and fortune.' Her eyes narrowed. 'If you think you'll be getting any money from me, *mademoiselle*, think again. Maybe I wasn't careful enough the first time I tried to deal with you but I will not be making *that* mistake again.'

'Are you *threatening* me?'

'I am giving you some advice. Go back to the village you came from and do not ever come here again.'

Alice's inward breath was a gasp of horror. 'Jacquot is my *brother*...'

'No.' The word was final. 'Jacques Laurent is my grandchild. My *only* grandchild. You...' The rings on her hand flashed again in a gesture that could have been used to brush dust from a polished surface. 'You are *rien. Nothing.*'

'You don't care a jot about him,' Alice hissed. 'You haven't even *looked* at him since you came into this house.'

Madame Laurent's eyebrows rose just a little. Enough to suggest a refined astonishment.

'The child will have the best care that money can provide. And I will raise him to be as much of a credit to the Laurent name as his father was.'

Alice let out a long breath. 'I wish I'd met my father,' she said slowly. 'I wish I could have thanked him for making sure I didn't grow up here—with you as my grandmother. I was genuinely loved and that…that is of far more value than anything money can buy.'

The moment's silence was brief.

'Have my grandson ready to travel by tomorrow afternoon. And be ready to leave yourself. I do not wish to see you again.'

And with that, Madame Laurent turned and left the nursery, having not taken a step closer to Alice. Or any nearer the cot that contained her *only* grandchild.

Alice was shaking from head to toe as she did something that would probably be frowned on by any baby-care guides. She lifted a soundly sleeping infant so that she could hold him in her arms and press her cheek gently against his downy head.

'I won't let it happen,' she whispered. 'I love you. Your uncle Julien loves you too, I know he does…and…and I love *him*…and I wouldn't have fallen in love with anyone who could let this happen so I know that you will be safe…'

* * *

Alice came downstairs as Madame Laurent's car was on its way to the front gates.

She looked pale. Shocked even.

Yvonne Laurent had looked a little pale herself when she'd come down a few minutes ago but that was understandable. To be presented with a relationship to an adult was a very different thing from meeting a vulnerable child and they would both need time.

And it wasn't really his business, was it? Nothing had changed. On leaving, Madame Laurent had only confirmed that she would be here tomorrow afternoon with their agreement legally documented.

So he smiled at Alice.

'All is well that ends well—is that how you say it?'

'Sorry?'

'A good result. I did not expect Yvonne Laurent to be so understanding. To agree to more than I had requested, in fact.'

'I…I don't understand…'

Alice had stopped moving. She sank down and sat very still, staring at him.

'There will be no need to go to court. She has agreed that I will be a part of Jaquot's life. That I will see him regularly and that, in the future, when she is no longer able to devote her life to her grandson, I will become his guardian.'

'Devote her life to him?' Alice looked horrified. 'Are you *kidding*? She doesn't care a jot for him, Julien. I don't think she even loved her own son. She wouldn't even *look* at Jacquot and she certainly isn't going to acknowledge me as his sister. She's an evil woman, can't you *see* that? She said the most horrible things about my mother. About *me*...'

The anguish in Alice's eyes was unbearable and it was too much like the kind of pain Julien had seen in other eyes, so long ago. It wasn't something he could fix and it might make things worse if he tried. To get too involved would only bring pain and hadn't he caused enough of that already? He was still too raw to cope with fresh wounds. He hadn't been able to protect Colette so what made him think he could help Alice?

At least he had protected Jacquot to the best of his ability.

And he could protect himself. He could feel himself turning inwards already, in search of that safe place.

'I expect that communication was difficult. Perhaps she wasn't able to express herself very well in your language.'

'Her English was perfect,' Alice said. 'Better than yours.'

If anything, her gaze was more intense now. 'You love Jacquot. You can't let this happen to him.'

She was looking at him the way she had when he'd told her so much about his childhood. As if she wanted to wave her magic wand and make him feel better.

Make him feel loved…

He couldn't go there. He didn't want to feel loved because that's how it all started. The need to give back. To love in return and to give everything you had. Then all you could do was wait for the inevitable pain when it got ripped away from you.

Just a few more steps and he could be in that safe place again. Couldn't Alice understand?

'You make everything about love,' he said. 'But that gets in the way of thinking with your head and not your heart and that's a dangerous path where too many people get hurt. Yes, my heart knows I love Jacquot but my head knows that what has been arranged is best. For everyone.'

Alice's eyes were huge in her pale face. 'You're afraid to take that path but you know that's what really matters. For everybody. *Especially* Jacquot...'

Her heart was breaking. She could feel it happening and the pain was unbearable.

The barriers were there again and more solid than ever.

The doubts she'd had during that awful time of waiting in the nursery surfaced again and this time they had vicious claws.

Julien had never said he loved her. He'd never even hinted that their time together would continue. He'd given her this special day because he'd known it was going to be their last and…and he'd been relieved when it was over. Look at the way the pleasure had been sucked out of the day when the woman at the hat stall had suggested they were a real family.

The spell had been broken then and now it was no more than a little sparkly dust. It would take no more than a heartfelt sigh to send that dust into oblivion.

He'd told her all along that it wasn't real. That it wasn't simply his work that stopped him from being able to raise a child. That he didn't *want* to…

Was there any point in trying to tell him that Jacquot's grandmother was an evil monster? What could she do? He'd been offered the perfect solution in which he could stay in that safe place he'd invented. The place where he didn't have to take the risk of truly loving.

Or being loved.

It was so obvious that Alice had reached the end of the road. That she was defeated.

'It makes no difference that I'm his sister, does it? That I can love him with all my heart and soul?'

That I could love you like that, too...

But she couldn't tell Julien that she loved him because he didn't *want* to be loved. Being rejected by Madame Laurent was one thing. To invite rejection from Julien was another thing entirely. Why make this even worse for herself?

And he wasn't going to tell her that he loved *her* because…because he didn't. It was that simple. He didn't know how to. She'd been right. She'd been no more than a distraction during a difficult time.

'I know you love Jacquot.' Julien's tone softened. 'And I…'

Something flashed in his eyes. It was a fleeting glimpse through the barriers. An echo of the 'thing'—that extraordinary connection they had found with each other. Oh, God…had she been wrong? Was he going to say that he loved *her*?

That would change everything. They could fight this together. And *win*…

'And I must thank you for everything that you've done for him.'

The disappointment was crushing. Why did she keep buying into that fairy-tale when she should know better by now? Alice dropped her gaze so that Julien wouldn't see her pain.

'Maybe, one day, I can arrange for you to see him again but, for now, things must be as they are. *Je suis désolé.*'

Alice stared at her hands. It was really over.

'I'm sorry, too,' she whispered. 'More than you'll ever know.'

Julien was moving away. Towards the grand salon. Towards her father's office perhaps?

'I have to speak to my solicitor. Madame Laurent is returning tomorrow and it might be easier for you if you are not in the house. I will arrange for someone to come and care for Jacques until I get back from Paris. Marthe perhaps. And I will see if a flight can be arranged to take you home. Would you prefer to fly into Glasgow or Edinburgh?'

Alice pushed herself to her feet and turned her back as she prepared to head back upstairs. Her response felt strangled. Like her heart.

'Edinburgh.'

It was so late by the time he had all the arrangements in place there was no time for anything more than another strong cup of coffee, a shower and a change of clothes before his taxi would arrive to get him to his early flight to Paris.

Julien left the printout of the plane ticket to Edinburgh he had finally managed to secure on the kitchen table where Alice would find it when she came down for breakfast. He had also printed out the voucher for the taxi that would come and collect her. Marthe would be here by then and he would be getting on his return flight from Paris. By the time he was landing in Nice, her plane would have just taken off. They would both be in the sky at the same time, but flying in very different directions.

He would never see her again.

Along with the ticket and taxi voucher, Julien left the colour image he had used the technology in André's office to print. The photograph of Alice, with Jacquot in her arms, at the Christmas market in Nice.

He owed her at least a small memento.

No. He owed her much more than that but if he began to count then it would only make everything more difficult. More painful.

The picture said it all. That this time had been pretence. No more than a Christmas time fairytale and real life wasn't like that.

Could he leave without saying goodbye?

No. Of course he couldn't. The force that was still pulling him towards this extraordinary young woman was too overwhelming to even begin resisting and surely he could cope. He just needed to peep through the window of his safe place—he didn't have to step outside it.

There was no sound coming from the nursery but the door was ajar and there was the soft glow of a nightlight to be seen. Julien pushed the door open a little further but then he stopped, his planned speech of farewell and thanks evaporating.

He'd heard Jacquot crying when he'd been downstairs and again when he was getting out of his shower but now the baby was a silent bundle in the cot and Alice was curled up in the chair asleep with her head in the crook of her arm. Her hair was a tangle of curls and her face looked as if tears had dried to leave streaks.

If he woke her, would she cry again?

And, if she did, would he be able to stop himself taking her into his arms and holding her close to his heart?

Buying into that dream again for just a few moments longer? Making those promises he knew he had no hope of keeping? Making things worse for them both in the long run?

It was the hardest thing he'd ever done, turning to walk silently away from that room, but it was best that he did.

Best that he focused on what he had to do in a matter of only a few hours, which was to present to the world the face of a man whose absolute passion was his career. A career that might once have seemed as much of a fairy-tale as a happy family but was reality.

And he had to hang onto that for all it was worth.

Because, when all was said and done, it was all he really had to count on.

CHAPTER ELEVEN

JULIEN HAD GONE.

Alice knew that she and Jacquot were alone in the house from the moment she awoke.

Because it felt like a part of herself was missing.

The part she had given to Julien…

Jacquot was still asleep after a fretful night, probably due to the distress he must have sensed in her, so she moved slowly and quietly around the nursery, her feet feeling as heavy as her heart. After a brief shower she packed her few items into the backpack she had arrived with. The photo of her parents—now more precious than ever—was tucked carefully back into the side pocket. The action reminded her of the photograph she'd found in André's office of Jacquot's parents and her vow to find some way to give it to him one day. She needed to remember to go and fetch it.

It was still dark well after the baby stirred and Alice gave him his breakfast bottle and then bathed and dressed him. She gave him extra kisses and cuddles this morning and talked to him.

'I'll find you one day, sweetheart. I expect you'll learn to speak English and I'm going to take French lessons, so by the time I see you again we'll be able to talk to each other.'

She thought of all the baby milestones Jacquot would have in the next few years, like saying his first words and taking his first wobbly steps. The pain of knowing she wouldn't be able to witness or celebrate those milestones was astonishingly painful.

She'd found what she'd come to France in the hope of finding. Someone that was family to her. Jacquot had accepted her from the moment they'd met. Even now, the memory of how she'd been the only one able to comfort him when he'd been sick and miserable brought a smile to her lips.

One that twisted in what felt like grief as she acknowledged that this gift of family was going to be wrenched from her in a matter of just a few hours.

And Julien hadn't even said goodbye.

The tears would come, nothing was surer, but Alice wasn't going to let it happen in the scant time she had left with her little brother. So she pasted a smile on her face.

'Shall we go downstairs, darling? So that Alice can have a cup of coffee?'

There would be no warm, buttery croissants ready for her this morning but it didn't matter. She couldn't have eaten anything anyway. Her stomach already felt like a stone and that stone became a painful boulder when she walked into the kitchen to find what had been left on the table for her.

The note was written in elegant handwriting. She could actually see Julien's hand holding the pen as she picked it up. Those long, clever fingers that were capable of magic in the kitchen. And in the bedroom…

Marthe would be arriving at ten-thirty a.m., the note informed her. Half an hour before her taxi was due to arrive to take her to the airport.

'Merci, chérie,' the brief note ended. *'Au revoir.'*

Au revoir. One of the language lessons over a meal had been about saying goodbye. And this really meant goodbye. If you intended seeing someone again, you said something like *'à demain'.* Until tomorrow. Or *'à bientôt'.* Soon.

The endearment was probably automatic. Like a London cab driver calling you 'love'.

It meant nothing.

Except that wasn't true, was it? She'd seen a part of Julien Dubois that instinct told her very few other people saw.

That 'thing'. That connection they'd found when they'd looked at each other in the bathroom mirror that first night had been an attraction that went very much deeper than anything physical. She knew, beyond a shadow of a doubt, that Julien had felt it too. He was choosing to deny it. To run away.

And she understood. She might hate it but she

had thought about nothing else in the sleepless hours before she'd finally succumbed to exhaustion last night.

She had told him that he was too afraid to take the path of love and it was true. He was protecting his heart but who could blame him when he'd lost everybody he'd given his heart to? His father had abandoned him at an impressionable age. He'd said himself that small children understood more than you would think and that was why he wanted to spare Jacquot the insecurity of having people fighting over his custody.

His mother had died at another impressionable age, when he'd been in that awkward transition period between child and adult, but he'd been mature enough to take responsibility for his young sister and devote his life to supporting and protecting her. Alice wasn't sure what had happened in recent years but the rift when he'd tried to protect Colette from marrying someone he hadn't trusted had to have been devastating. And just when it had looked like they were about to reconnect, he had lost his sister under tragic circumstances that were still raw.

No wonder he couldn't offer anyone else a part of his heart to keep for ever. There weren't that many parts left. And yet he'd tried, with Jacquot. He had been fighting to at least be a meaningful part of his nephew's life the day she had arrived here. There'd been an enforced disruption to the negotiations thanks to the quarantine but now he had exactly what he'd intended fighting for.

He had no idea what Madame Laurent was really like and, in trying to tell him, she had only made the distance between them greater. Maybe he hadn't been able to hear what she'd had to say because, if he believed her, it would destroy the victory he thought he'd won. Maybe that was why he hadn't risked waking her to say goodbye?

Had he felt the connection with her that he'd been unable to deny when he'd printed out this photograph of her at the Christmas markets?

Or had he remembered, instead, the shock of that stallholder assuming they were the parents of the small baby in their company? A happy little family. That he had a child of his own when he'd vowed that he would never let that happen.

As if he knew his part in the fantasy, Jacquot reached up and caught the corner of the photograph in his small fist, crumpling it with surprising strength.

'Oops…' Alice gently extracted the glossy image. However painful it was in this moment, she was going to keep this. It didn't matter that it was now crumpled because she'd remember the tiny hand that had caused the damage and that made it even more precious.

She barely glanced at the plane ticket and taxi voucher because her intention of putting this photograph into her backpack beside the one of her parents had reminded her of the other photograph she was planning to take with her. The one in the heart-shaped, silver frame.

'Come on.' She smiled down at Jacquot, who now had a handful of her hair. 'Let's go to Daddy's office.'

She hadn't been in here since the night she'd interrupted the filming of the Christmas show that was probably being aired on television right now, with the hosts of the breakfast show chatting to Julien between clips. Was he wearing his white chef's tunic and that blue and white striped apron? Had it only been the night before last that he had emerged from the kitchen to kiss her senseless and give her the most memorable night of her life?

Such a contrast to the first memorable moment he'd given her, when he'd hurled that paperweight at her father's massive portrait. She stood in front of it for a long moment, ignoring the shards of glass and even the reason for the photograph. Instead, she looked into her father's eyes. Dark eyes, so like her own, that gleamed with such confidence and joy.

A man capable of great passion. Like Julien. But her father hadn't been afraid to love more than his career. He'd loved Colette, she was sure of that. Picking up the photograph in the silver frame only convinced her more. She clicked it shut. She was going to believe that André Laurent had loved *her* mother, too. He had been a victim of his upbringing perhaps. Overindulged and dependent financially on a woman who had no heart.

It was more of a stretch to believe that he'd helped Jeanette to escape the planned termination of her pregnancy but maybe her mother had severed contact so completely he'd known there was no point in trying to find her. The birth of his son at such a late age must have been a miracle. How sad that it had come at such a price, though. Had he been distraught? Had that contributed to his reckless driving that had taken his life?

He hadn't intended to die. Sinking into the desk chair, Alice used her free hand to open the drawer she'd opened the last time she had been in here. Yes. There were the tickets and passports ready to take Jacquot to his grandmother's house for his first Christmas.

Alice actually shuddered at the thought of being in that woman's company for anything, let alone a celebration like Christmas.

It was just as well she wasn't going to be here this afternoon to see Jacquot handed over to a woman who had no love in her soul. The family name was all Madame Laurent cared about, not the person who was carrying that name.

A flash of anger cut through weariness that went bone-deep.

How could Julien even think of allowing that to happen?

Maybe he wasn't the person she thought he was. Maybe she'd invented a prince for her fairy-tale and then she'd been stupid enough to fall in love with him.

No. In her heart of hearts she knew that wasn't true. Julien didn't know the truth or he would not let this happen. Nobody would.

Her arms tightened around Jacquot as she ducked her head to plant a kiss on his head. She'd promised this tiny person that she wouldn't let it happen. That his Uncle Julien wouldn't let it happen. But…but…

Alice blinked tears away as she raised her head, her glance grazing the drawer and its contents again as she did so.

Unbidden, her hand went out to pick up one of the items.

Jacquot's passport.

The idea was ludicrous. An act of rebellion that would get her into far more trouble than any of her childhood pranks.

But it wasn't impossible, was it?

Marthe wasn't coming here for another few hours. She had a voucher for the taxi company that included a phone number. If they spoke English—as most people seemed to here—she could change the time of her pick-up.

She had a plane ticket. A three-month-old baby didn't need a plane ticket because it got held in its mother's arms.

And who was going to check whether she actually was his mother? It was Christmas Eve and bound to be bedlam at any international airport.

She could keep Jacquot safe even if it was only for a short time before she was caught. She could keep him safe for his first-ever Christmas. Make him feel wanted and loved for no more than who he was. Her brother.

The idea was growing wings. The mix of nervousness and excitement felt rather like when she'd first arrived here. It would take courage to do it because she knew how wrong it was.

But then she looked down at a tiny face and Jacquot looked back and her and grinned his crooked little grin.

No. It wasn't wrong. It wasn't exactly the right thing to do either.

It was the *only* thing to do.

The airport was so chaotic Julien didn't remember to turn his phone back on until he'd finally managed to flag down a taxi and was stuck in the crazy Christmas traffic as he headed back to St Jean Cap Ferrat.

Ten missed calls from Marthe?

He knew his heart actually stopped for a moment because he felt the painful thump of it restarting.

Something had happened to Jacquot.
Or Alice.

His fingers shook as he tapped the screen to return the call. A moment later the housekeeper's voice was a distressed garble.

'I don't understand. Of course Alice has gone. Her plane will have taken off by now.'

He'd seen a British Airways plane taking off as he'd hurried through the crowds to escape the airport and he'd wondered if that was Alice disappearing from his life for ever. It had only made it more urgent to escape. To do what had to be done and then retreat into the only life he knew he could depend on. His own.

He was only half listening to Marthe's next words.

'How could she have taken Jacquot with her? You were there when the taxi came.'

He closed his eyes as he listened to the explanation. The taxi company had been and gone by the time Marthe had arrived at the house. Alice had left a note to say not to worry but the plan had been changed. That Julien would know why. So she'd been trying to ring him. Again and again.

But his phone had been turned off. Of course it had. He couldn't afford to have it ring when he was on a live television show and he hadn't bothered turning it back on when he had been about to fly.

If Alice had been on that plane he'd seen taking off, she hadn't been alone. She was taking her little brother back to Edinburgh and from there to whatever isolated little village she came from. What was its name? She had told him once. It would come to him.

Right now, the enormity of what had happened was sinking in as his taxi cleared the worst of the traffic and picked up speed. There was only an hour or two at most before Yvonne Laurent arrived to collect Jacquot and when she found out what had happened all hell would break loose. Would she think that he'd had a part in this himself? Would it send them all back to square one in a battle for Jacquot's custody?

How long did it take to fly to Edinburgh? No more than three hours, he suspected. Time enough for the full force of the law to be unleashed. Alice would be arrested the moment she arrived. Prosecution by the Laurent solicitors would be relentless and unforgiving. Jacquot would be taken away from her and brought back to France by strangers. He would be frightened and that was enough to make Julien angry. Very, very angry.

How could she do that?

What had she been *thinking*?

There was no reason for Marthe to stay in the house. Julien sent her home to her family. He screwed up the note Alice had left and hurled it to the floor of the kitchen. And then he began pacing, still unable to believe what she had done. He went in the direction of the nursery, as though he had to see for himself that it was uninhabited.

Which, of course, it was.

There was no sign that Alice had even been here but the absence of the baby whose name was proclaimed in those bright wooden letters on the wall was horrific.

The cot had been neatly made and propped against the soft bumper pad at the head end was a toy.

Le lapin brun.

Somehow that was even more shocking than Jacquot's absence. Alice had known how precious this toy was. She had said herself that she was happy it was there for him. That, one day, Julien would be able to tell him how special it was. How much he must have been loved.

He had to pick it up and, as he did so he remembered the last time he'd reached into this cot. When he'd been half-asleep and half-dressed and had gone into the nursery in response to that alarming cry from Jacquot.

And he remembered how he'd felt, holding that tiny baby against his bare chest. The pride in being able to comfort him. The absolute trust he was being endowed with to protect this baby from any evil in the world.

He could hear a whisper that sounded like Alice's voice.

She doesn't care a jot for him…I don't think she even loved her own son… She's an evil woman, can't you see that?

Alice had felt that same level of trust from Jacquot, hadn't she? And she'd been brave enough to do something about it, however ill advised that had been. Anger was fading now, being replaced with something that felt more like respect. Admiration even.

But now Julien had the battered old bunny in his hand and he remembered the feel of it as if it was only yesterday that he had been handing it to his little sister to comfort her. How she would take it and clutch it to her chest and then wriggle into his arms to be held and comforted some more.

And finally…having not cried since his father had walked out when he'd been only five years old—even when his stepfather had beaten him or when his mother had died, leaving a scared youth to try and fight back against an unfair world—Julien was able to cry for his sister.

Racking sobs that felt like they were tearing his heart apart as he sank into the chair he'd seen Alice asleep in only this morning. Tears that soaked the toy he had pressed against his cheek. But curiously the pain didn't seem to be destroying what was left of his heart. When he was finally spent, there was an odd calmness to be found.

The beginning of peace perhaps?

It was only then that Julien became aware of something in the chair he'd been sitting in. Something with uncomfortably sharp edges. He reached underneath his legs and pulled out the handset to the baby monitor. Its red light was glowing but there was no point in keeping it on when there was no baby to watch over, was there?

Julien pushed a button but the light stayed on. He pushed another one and, unexpectedly, an image filled the screen. Did this state-of-the-art baby monitoring equipment actually make a video recording when it was switched on?

Apparently it did.

And the last time it had been switched on had been last evening. When Yvonne Laurent had gone up to the nursery after receiving the shocking news that there were *two* grandchildren of hers in the room.

He watched—and listened—in growing horror. Was this really the same woman whose words and tears had convinced him that they shared the same dream for Jacquot's future?

'The arrangements had been made. I had paid their exorbitant fees myself so that the unfortunate pregnancy could be dealt with discreetly.'

'...a waitress—who'd been stupid enough to try and catch him by producing an unwanted brat...'

'Jacques Laurent is my grandchild. My only grandchild... You... You are rien. *Nothing.'*

How hurtful must that have been? Words could hurt just as much as fists and he knew only too well what it was like to feel so unwanted. Rejected.

His little Scottish pixie had come here wanting nothing more than to find family in time for Christmas.

She'd found that her father had died only days before.

She'd found a tiny brother she could love and she'd been desperate to be allowed to raise him herself.

And she'd ended up being dismissed as *nothing*.

The anger was there again now but it wasn't directed at Alice. When the vicious old woman that his nephew was unfortunate enough to have as a grandmother arrived he was going to tell her exactly how wrong she was about Alice McMillan. Nothing? She was *everything* that Yvonne Laurent could clearly never be. Warm. Loving. Vibrant. Able to make life something to be celebrated, no matter what.

And...

Julien caught his breath as he focused on the small screen again. What was that? He studied the buttons on the handset properly this time so he could rewind and play that part again that he'd barely noticed during his outraged thoughts.

'I love you. Your uncle Julien loves you too, I know he does...and...and I love him...and I wouldn't have fallen in love with anyone who could let this happen...'

Mon Dieu...

The cascade of emotion was enough to bring tears to his eyes again but these were not tears of grief.

They felt more like joy.

And then Julien heard the doorbell ring. It was

probably his solicitor, who was due to arrive before Madame Laurent in order to check that the
legal paperwork was irrefutable. Paperwork that
would now need to be ripped into shreds.

He got to his feet, the brown bunny in one hand
and the handset of the monitor in the other.

Alice had left him one final gift, hadn't she?

The weapon he needed to win this battle, once
and for all.

No. Make that two.

Unintentionally, she had also given him words
of love.

Would they still hold true when he'd dismissed
what she'd told him about that encounter with her
grandmother? When he'd done what must have
seemed so unforgiveable in her eyes? When he'd
turned away from her so deliberately in order to
protect himself?

There was only one way to find out.

But there were other matters to attend to first.

It was dark by the time the plane landed at Edinburgh airport even though it was only three p.m.

Leaden skies held the weight of a snowstorm that everyone was hoping would hold off for at least twenty-four hours to give families time to gather for Christmas.

In rural Scotland, well to the north, it was already snowing. Tiny flakes sparkled in the headlights of her rented car as Alice finally parked in front of the cottage that had been her home since the day she was born.

The home she had celebrated every single Christmas in, with the decorations her mother had loved strung from every available anchoring point, a tree with flashing fairy-lights and gifts underneath, a fire burning brightly in the grate, Christmas carols coming from the CD player and the smell of a feast being prepared in the kitchen.

Home...

Jacquot was asleep in the car seat she had also rented. She carried him into the small stone house.

A very cold and dark stone house.

Aside from her brief visit back here last week, nobody had been living here for many months and there was no power on. No fire in the grate. Probably very little food in the pantry even. The shops would be shut and she didn't even have a close neighbour she could call on. There was no Christmas tree, no decorations and no music.

It was so quiet she could hear her own heart beating.

Until Jacquot woke and started to cry.

Alice undid the safety harness and scooped him into her arms. She wanted to cry herself.

What had she done?

What had she been *thinking*?

CHAPTER TWELVE

CHRISTMAS MORNING.

Somehow they'd survived the night.

Leaving Jacquot cocooned in blankets, tucked into the car seat that doubled as a carrier, Alice had used the light of her phone to find candles and then she'd built a fire in the ancient Aga stove in the kitchen that her grandmother had insisted on keeping because she'd been cooking on it ever since she'd come here as a young bride. At the same time she started a fire going in the open grate of the only living area in the house.

Feeding Jacquot was no problem now that she had a means of heating water because she had packed plenty of formula into the nappy bag, along with everything else she might need for a baby for a few days. She must have looked a sight at Nice airport yesterday, with her backpack on, a baby strapped to her chest and a well-stuffed carrier bag in each hand, but she'd been right in guessing that officials had been too busy to ask awkward questions. Instead, she'd found people eager to help a struggling young mother who'd had too many burdens to juggle. She'd got priority boarding and had been allowed to take all her bags onto the plane instead of checking any in, which had made for a much faster get-away when they'd arrived in Edinburgh.

That had been the worse time. The flight had been long enough for Alice to convince herself that Julien had arrived back in St Jean Cap Ferrat and would have been as furious as Madame Laurent to discover what she'd done. That the police would have been called. She had fully expected them to be waiting for her at Edinburgh airport.

But they hadn't been there.

And now she was several hours' drive away and, as if fate was lending her a helping hand, snow had fallen heavily all night. With any luck, it would take at least until tomorrow for roads to be clear enough to access Brannockburn easily.

She might not have the luxury of a few days' grace but it felt like she could count on having today.

Christmas Day.

And that was what mattered, wasn't it? This was Jacquot's first Christmas and she wanted it to be filled with all the love it was possible for a family to share. All the magic of Christmas.

Except there was nothing that said 'Christmas' about this house, except for the candles that she'd lit again once she was up for the day.

It was warm now, thank goodness. Rather than using the bedrooms upstairs, Alice had slept on the couch all night, getting up to look after Jacquot, who had slept in his nest of blankets, and stoking the fires each time.

But there was no tree. No decorations and no music. And certainly no smell of anything delicious being prepared in the kitchen—only the faint reminder of the can of baked beans Alice had heated for her breakfast.

They needed a tree.

'When I was little,' she told Jacquot, 'we all

used to put our wellies on and go out to the big old pine tree beside the henhouse. I was allowed to choose the branch and Mum would saw it off. We had a red bucket full of sand that we kept on the back porch beside the firewood pile and we stood the branch up in that.'

The red bucket was still there. She'd seen it last night when she'd hurried in and out with arm-loads of small logs to fill the indoor basket.

She tickled Jacquot's tummy as he lay on the cushion of folded blankets, kicking his legs, and he grinned up at her.

With Julien's grin…

No…she couldn't go there… She wasn't going to cry today. Not on Christmas Day. She needed a distraction. Fast.

'What do you think, sweetheart? Shall we do it? If we were very quick, and chose a branch close to the ground, it wouldn't take long enough for us to get *too* cold because it's not snowing at the moment. And I know where the decorations are—in the boxes under Gran's bed. We won't be able to have the fairy-lights and I'm sorry I don't have any gifts for you but…but we could still make it *feel* right and I can take photos so that, one day, you'll know how special your sister wanted to make your first Christmas.'

There was another bonus to her plan. It would take most of the day to do everything she was suddenly desperate to do and it would stop her sitting around, thinking about Julien. The hardest moment came when she realised she needed a hat before she went tramping around in the snow and the only hat she had was the one Julien had bought for her at the markets in Nice. She pulled it over her head anyway.

'It's Christmas,' she told Jacquot, as she slipped her arms into the straps of the front pack. 'We need all the sparkles we can find.'

The daylight hours had come and gone in a flash. Here it was, four p.m., and it felt like night-time. Alice pulled the curtains over the windows to keep the warmth inside and she could see the starry shapes of fresh snowflakes sticking to the dark glass and piling up on the windowsills.

She was cutting them off from the outside world but it felt good. This was a private celebration and, as she turned and caught the full effect of the living room, it was perfect enough to make her catch her breath.

Okay, the hastily harvested tree branch was lopsided but it didn't matter because it was staying upright in the red bucket. And it didn't matter that it didn't have sparkling lights because it was plastered with every bauble Alice had found in the old boxes and with so many candles on the old sideboard and the mantelpiece, as well as the firelight, the glossy decorations were twinkling anyway.

Garlands of fake spruce and ivy, generously sprinkled with bunches of red berries, were looped above the doorways and from the heavy beams in the ceiling.

The beautiful stockings that her grandmother had lovingly embroidered were hanging above the fire and Alice had put tiny tea-light candles in glass tumblers on the hearth. The huge wickerwork reindeer her mother had loved stood guard on either side of the fireplace, proudly wearing their red collars and golden bells.

It didn't matter that there were no gifts under the tree either. Jacquot was too young to know the difference and Alice had the best gift she could possibly have already.

Family.

'We need a photo,' she told her tiny brother. 'I've never done a selfie before but here goes.'

She was wearing a Santa hat she'd found amongst the decorations and she'd dressed Jacquot in a little red sleep suit she'd packed with his things. Standing in front of the tree, with the baby tucked into the crook of one arm, Alice used her other hand to try and hold her phone far enough away to capture both their faces and some of the background.

It wasn't working. If she tilted the phone enough to put Jacquot's face in the picture, it cut off the top half of her own head and the tree was nowhere to be seen. 'I give up,' she sighed finally. 'I'll just take a picture of you and then we'll use my phone to have some Christmas music.'

The battery was not going to last much longer so Alice had to choose a favourite carol to listen to while she prepared Jacquot's Christmas dinner of a bottle of milk.

With the much-loved sound of 'The Little Drummer Boy' playing, she cuddled Jacquot for a minute longer, singing softly along with the song.

And then she froze.

No...it couldn't be...

But then she heard it again.

An insistent rapping on the front door of her house. Her time with Jacquot was about to end.

She'd been caught. It was time to face music that would have none of the joy of any Christmas carols.

She kept her head down as she opened her door, expecting to see the polished boots of more than one police officer.

She did see boots but they were old and soft looking, like a favourite pair a cowboy might wear. And they were beneath a pair of faded denim jeans. Alice's head jerked up.

'*Julien*...'

* * *

She had been hunted down by the person she was most ashamed to see and she could feel her face flood with burning colour as she thought of how much trouble she must have caused him.

But he was smiling. *'Bonjour, Alice. Joyeux Noël.* May I come inside?'

Speechless as she absorbed the sound of his voice again, Alice could only nod as she stood back. He was carrying a suitcase in one hand. No…it wasn't a case, she realised as he came into the light of the living room. It looked like…like a *picnic* hamper?

And he was holding something in his other hand as well.

Brown bunny.

Julien saw the direction of her gaze and held up the toy.

'I think you forgot something,' he said softly, holding it out to her. 'Something important.'

Her hand was trembling as she took the toy and she still couldn't think of a single word to say. This was the last thing she'd expected. Why wasn't he furious? Berating her for the crime she had committed in kidnapping Jacquot? Snatching him from her arms and disappearing back into the gloomy chill of the dark, snowy afternoon?

Finally, she found her voice, already sounding rusty. 'How did you find me? How did you *get* here?'

'I remembered the name of your village. Getting here was a little more problematic, especially when my car got stuck in the snow, but a very nice man with a tractor rescued me and, even better, he knew where your house was. I have walked the last mile or so. My feet are very cold.'

'Oh…come over near the fire.'

'Soon.' Julien put the hamper down and took off his coat. Then he pulled the hat off his head and the hair that had been tucked out of sight fell softly to touch his shoulders.

He stepped closer. 'You have forgotten something else. Or maybe you didn't know about it.' He bent to kiss Jacquot's head and then touched Alice's cheek with equal gentleness as he met her gaze.

She couldn't look away. The 'thing' was still there but it had changed. Grown. In fact, it was so huge it seemed to be sucking all the oxygen out of this room. Not that it mattered because she was too stunned to think about taking a breath anyway.

His hand traced her cheek, brushed her ear and then slid beneath her hair to cup the back of her head. Alice's lips were already slightly parted as she looked up, her heart so full of love it felt painfully stretched, and Julien matched his own lips with hers so perfectly it was like a dance as much as a kiss as they moved together.

'It is a French custom,' he whispered. 'The Christmas kiss.'

Vision blurred by tears made Alice blink. She couldn't believe any of this. It was a dream. A fairy-tale. Real life wasn't like this.

Except, right now, it appeared that it was.

Julien was stepping back. He picked up the hamper. 'There was so much food still in the cold room,' he said, 'I thought I would bring you Christmas dinner.'

Alice had thought that the traditional meal was the one thing she had needed to complete this Christmas celebration for Jacquot. But, in the wave of a magic wand, it had now appeared and she knew she'd been wrong.

What she had really needed to complete this perfect little Christmas was to be with both the people she now thought of as family.

Jacquot *and* Julien.

A single tear escaped and trickled down her cheek.

Miracles really did happen at Christmastime, didn't they?

'I have champagne, too,' Julien added. 'Because we have something to celebrate.'

'We do?'

'*Oui*. But first I must apologise. I had no idea about the terrible things Madame Laurent said to you. I had no idea what sort of person she really was because, I think, her acting skills are excellent. I should have listened. I will always listen in future, *mon amour. Je suis vraiment désolé.*'

That French was being spoken in this house, of

all places, should have felt like a betrayal to her grandmother and mother but instead it felt like the two halves of who she was had finally been fitted together like a jigsaw puzzle. Or maybe she was feeling whole because Julien was here with her. Whatever the reason, the picture that the neatly fitting pieces were making was beautiful.

Jacquot's whimper reminded her that it was time for him to be fed but Alice hesitated. The shock of seeing Julien was wearing off and questions were filling her head. Serious questions.

'How do you know what she said? Did she *tell* you? Why? And where is she now? What's going to happen to me?'

Julien smiled. 'One question at a time, *mon amour*. Here, give Jacquot to me or would you like me to prepare his bottle?'

In answer, Alice transferred the bundle of baby from her arms to his and Jacquot, bless him, looked up at his uncle and forgot he was hungry. He practised his best smile instead. Julien followed Alice to the kitchen and watched as she reheated the pot of boiled water on the hotplate over the oven.

'Did you know that the baby cam could record things?'

'No.' Alice spooned formula into the bottle. If she had, she might have gone back to watch a particular scene more than once. The one where Julien had picked up his tiny nephew and held him against his bare chest. A scene that had captured her heart so decisively.

'It was lucky that you'd turned it on before Madame Laurent came into the nursery. It recorded everything she said.'

Alice's eyes widened. 'That's right…I'd turned it on because I'd been about to come downstairs and find you…'

'It gave me the evidence I needed to confront her. My solicitor reminded her that what she had done had been ill advised and illegal if your mother had been more than twelve weeks pregnant. That, in any case, if this recording became public, her reputation would be ruined and if she contested the issue of guardianship any further, then that was exactly what would happen.'

Alice gasped. 'She must have been *so* angry.'

Julien nodded, a sombre expression on his face. 'So angry the doctors said later that it must have raised her blood pressure to a terrible level and that is why she had the…I don't know the word… *un accident vasculaire cerebral…*'

'A stroke?' Alice guessed, shocked. 'Oh, my God… Is she…is she still alive?'

Julien nodded again. 'But she is badly affected. I rang the hospital this morning before I left to check on her progress and it is thought she will need specialist care for a long time.'

Alice absorbed this information slowly as she shook the bottle and then tested the temperature of the formula on her wrist.

'So she can't take Jacquot even if she wanted to fight for custody?'

'No. My guardianship will be uncontested. Ironically, that was part of our agreement that she had already signed. That if anything happened to her, this is what would happen. From now on, he will be in my care.'

Alice nodded slowly, trying to take it all in. So that was why Julien had come instead of the police. He was here to take Jacquot back to France with him.

'Would...?' She had to clear her throat so her voice didn't wobble. 'Would you like to feed him?'

'You give Jacquot his dinner.' Julien gently transferred the baby back to her arms. 'I would like to give you *your* dinner and I need to make it hot.' He was smiling now. 'Do you remember the last Christmas dinner we ate together?'

How could she forget, when it had happened after he had taken her to his bed for the first time? By the look in his eyes right now he was remembering exactly the same thing.

'And do you remember I said you might be eating Christmas dinner more than once?'

Alice's knees felt a little weak. Was Julien referring to a repetition of more than eating a traditional meal? She needed to sit down while she fed Jacquot, who fell asleep before he had even finished his milk.

And then Julien brought her a glass of champagne and sat beside her on the old couch as they drank it. Silently, they sat together, soaking in the warmth and light of this Christmas scene Alice had created today.

'You really are a pixie,' Julien told her finally. 'You make the world a special place wherever you are.'

He took her empty glass and put it on the coffee table with his and then he put his arm around her and Alice snuggled against him, tilting her face up to receive one kiss and then another. They couldn't go upstairs to a bedroom and leave a baby in a room with a fire and a dozen candles but, unexpectedly, this felt better than sex. Deeper.

More like real life instead of a fairy-tale?

'Why did you leave *le lapin brun* behind?' Julien asked softly. 'Did you know I would find it?'

Alice nodded, loving the feel of Julien's chest beneath her cheek. She could hear his heart beating.

'I hoped so,' she said. 'I knew how much it meant to you. That it was the one thing Colette had given her baby that had been hers from her childhood. It was the link...the *love*...and I hoped that one day you would be able to give it to Jacquot so that the chain of that love wouldn't be broken.'

'Colette used to hold it when she was frightened.' Julien's voice cracked as he spoke. 'And I used to hold her. Like this...' His arm tightened around Alice and she snuggled closer.

'I'm not afraid to take the path of love,' he whispered, his lips very close to her ear. 'Not any more. I will love Jacquot for every day that I live and I will protect him in every way that I can.'

Alice pressed her lips together to stop them trembling. 'You will take him back to France?'

'I have to, *cherié*. You know that, yes?'

Alice nodded.

'But there is something I am also hoping...'

Alice tilted her head so that she could see his face.

'I am hoping that you will come back with us.

That you will help me raise Jacquot and give him the love that only his sister or mother could provide.'

Alice stopped breathing. Was that all Julien was hoping? His eyes were telling her more than that but was he really not afraid to take an even bigger step into trusting that he could not only give love but *be* loved in return?

'*Je t'aime*,' he whispered. '*Tu as volé mon coeur. Tu as changé mon vie et…je pense que tu es la dernière pièce de mon casse-tête.*'

Oh… Alice's eyes filled with joyous tears. Could there ever be a more beautiful language for words of love? She didn't need a translation.

Or maybe she did.

'What does that mean? What is a *casse-tête*?'

'A puzzle. I said that I think *you* are the last piece of *my* puzzle.'

'Oh…that's exactly what I was thinking about you. I… No… *Je t'aime*, too, Julien. I always will. For ever.'

'*Pour toujours*,' Julien confirmed. And then he kissed her, so tenderly that the tears in Alice's eyes escaped to dampen both their faces. Or had Julien shed some of his own?

The smell of the heating turkey and gravy wafted into the room at that point. Alice's stomach growled loudly and Julien tipped back his head as he laughed.

'I am home,' he declared. 'And it is time to feed my woman.'

He stood up, lifting Alice to her feet, but instead of leading her to the kitchen he wrapped his arms around her again.

'This is only the first of many,' he whispered. 'And I will try to make each one happier than the last. *Joyeux Noël, mon amour.*'

'*Joyeux Noël*,' Alice echoed. And then she stood on tiptoe so that she could kiss Julien again. 'It's a Scottish custom, too,' she murmured. 'The Christmas kiss…'

* * * * *

MILLS & BOON®
Large Print – February 2016

Claimed for Makarov's Baby
Sharon Kendrick

An Heir Fit for a King
Abby Green

The Wedding Night Debt
Cathy Williams

Seducing His Enemy's Daughter
Annie West

Reunited for the Billionaire's Legacy
Jennifer Hayward

Hidden in the Sheikh's Harem
Michelle Conder

Resisting the Sicilian Playboy
Amanda Cinelli

Soldier, Hero...Husband?
Cara Colter

Falling for Mr December
Kate Hardy

The Baby Who Saved Christmas
Alison Roberts

A Proposal Worth Millions
Sophie Pembroke

MILLS & BOON®
Large Print – March 2016

A Christmas Vow of Seduction
Maisey Yates

Brazilian's Nine Months' Notice
Susan Stephens

The Sheikh's Christmas Conquest
Sharon Kendrick

Shackled to the Sheikh
Trish Morey

Unwrapping the Castelli Secret
Caitlin Crews

A Marriage Fit for a Sinner
Maya Blake

Larenzo's Christmas Baby
Kate Hewitt

His Lost-and-Found Bride
Scarlet Wilson

Housekeeper Under the Mistletoe
Cara Colter

Gift-Wrapped in Her Wedding Dress
Kandy Shepherd

The Prince's Christmas Vow
Jennifer Faye